✔ KU-768-093

WITHDRAWN FROM STOCK

Diary of a
6th Grade
NINJA

Scavengers

WITHDRAWN FROM STOCK

Diary of a 6th Grade NINJA

BOOK 7
Scavengers

MARCUS EMERSON

ILLUSTRATED BY **DAVID LEE**

ALLEN&UNWIN
SYDNEY•MELBOURNE•AUCKLAND•LONDON

First published by Allen & Unwin in 2017

Copyright © Text, Marcus Emerson 2013
Copyright © Illustrations, David Lee 2013

All rights reserved. No part of this book may be reproduced or transmitted
in any form or by any means, electronic or mechanical, including photocopying,
recording or by any information storage and retrieval system, without prior
permission in writing from the publisher. The Australian *Copyright Act 1968*
(the Act) allows a maximum of one chapter or ten per cent of this book, whichever
is the greater, to be photocopied by any educational institution for its educational
purposes provided that the educational institution (or body that administers it) has
given a remuneration notice to the Copyright Agency (Australia) under the Act.

Allen & Unwin
83 Alexander Street
Crows Nest NSW 2065
Australia
Phone: (61 2) 8425 0100
Email: info@allenandunwin.com
Web: www.allenandunwin.com

A Cataloguing-in-Publication entry is available
from the National Library of Australia
www.trove.nla.gov.au

ISBN 978 1 76029 561 5

Cover design by Marcus Emerson and Sandra Nobes
Text design by Sandra Nobes
Cover and internal illustrations by David Lee
Set in 14 pt Adobe Garamond by Sandra Nobes
Printed in Australia by McPherson's Printing Group

7 9 10 8

www.marcusemerson.com

The paper in this book is FSC® certified.
FSC® promotes environmentally responsible,
socially beneficial and economically viable
management of the world's forests.

This one's for Oliver,
Emerson and Miles

So there I was falling into an ice volcano on Scrag Seven, one of Jupiter's moons, with about a hundred ice-ninjas trailing behind me. I couldn't say I knew I'd be fine when I jumped into the volcano, but I would say this – I was glad that I put on clean underwear that morning.

Oh, and don't for one second think I was in the middle of lunch, dreaming that insane scenario. That happened *one time* and suddenly I'm the dude who falls asleep all the time? C'mon, people! Does that sound like something I'd do?

Don't answer that.

My name is Chase Cooper, and I'm a sixth grade ninja...falling into an ice volcano on Scrag Seven.

The ice-ninjas had chased me across the frozen terrain of Scrag. They surprised me when I was rescuing a girl they had imprisoned named Gwen. She was also a sixth grader. I don't know how she managed to get herself caught on one of Jupiter's moons, but she did. She was cute too, and totally had the hots for me because I'm a way cool ninja.

As Gwen and I fell deeper into the volcano, I spun around in the air. I wasn't sure exactly how many ice-ninjas were after us, but I knew we were stupidly outnumbered, and the volcano floor was coming up fast.

'Chase!' Gwen shouted. 'The ground!'

I flipped over, grabbing Gwen's belt and pulling her closer. 'Hang on,' I said.

With my right leg, I spun a roundhouse kick so lightning fast that our descent instantly stopped centimetres from the ground, allowing me to set my feet down as if I were simply stepping off a staircase. *Science!*

'Whoa,' Gwen whispered, looking into my eyes. But her lovesick gaze quickly turned to fear as she looked above us. '*Look out!*'

From the reflection in her eyes, I could see a massive chunk of ice plummeting towards us. I pushed Gwen out of harm's way, totally saving her life at the last second like it was a movie.

If it was just the chunk of ice, we would've been in the clear, but that would've been too easy. The ice-ninjas were about to drop around us at any moment.

I sighed. 'Better stand back. It's about to get all kinds of hot in here.'

The thing about an army of ice-ninjas is that it doesn't take much to get rid of them. A simple flame would do, but being a fan of theatrics, I decide to go with something... bigger.

I brought my hands together like I was
holding a ball and curled my shoulders over
them. At that instant, a spark erupted in my
hands. I contained the spark, pushing it around
and around in my hands until it became a tiny
flame. Then I blew into the centre of the circle,
right on the small ball of fire I had created.

The itsy-bitsy ball of fire exploded, but
luckily, my ninja master had taught me how to
contain a blast like that. He also taught me
how to *throw* a blast like that.

Throwing both of my hands above Gwen
and me, I let the inferno surge from my
fingertips.

The ice-ninjas tried to stop their descent, but
it was too late. The ball of fire blew through

them, instantly melting their frozen bodies, sending them to their watery graves.

'How awful,' Gwen said as small drops of water rained down upon us.

'They're not real,' I said. 'Just frozen water that the Scrag queen cast a spell on. They feel neither pain nor remorse.'

'Still,' Gwen said. 'It's an awful fate.'

'Better than rotting away in an ice-prison,' I replied. Looking further into the volcano's cavern, I said, 'You've been here for a while now. Any idea where the queen is?'

When I looked at Gwen's face, she was staring at me. Not angry. Just staring.

Her voice became a whisper. 'Perhaps she's been with you the entire time...'

'What are you—' I stopped short when I turned around. The innocent girl I had rescued was standing before me, her eyes glowing white as her hair flapped in the cold wind of the cavern. 'Of course. My gut *told* me you couldn't be trusted.'

'Then why did you?' the queen asked, her voice sounding like several voices speaking at once.

I shrugged. 'I just thought I was hungry.'

The queen took a step towards me. Her foot sizzled on the icy floor of the volcano as the cave started to shake. Dust shook from the walls of the cavern, which meant the volcano was going to erupt...*soon*.

'I have to admit,' the queen hissed, 'you've made it *further* than I ever expected. I figured by this time, I'd be sitting in front of my fireplace with buttered toast and a steaming cup of hot chocolate.'

I thought the cave rumbled again, but it was just my stomach. Buttered toast and hot chocolate sounded *awesome*.

'Join me, Chase!' the queen said. 'Join me, and together we shall rule the human race!'

'Not a chance,' I said. 'I don't do well with public speaking, and if I ruled the human race, I'm sure I'd have to make, like, announcements and stuff.'

The queen's eyes glowed brighter. 'If you're not with me, you're against me!'

The light coming from the queen was so

blinding that I had to turn away. The
temperature in the cavern dropped about a
hundred degrees from cold to *way colder*. Any
bit of moisture in my breath froze the instant it
left my mouth, turning into microscopic specks
of ice that fell to the floor. That could happen
right? Yeah, that could *totally* happen.

The walls of the cavern shook again, this
time more violently. Huge chunks of ice broke
from the ceiling, smashing into the floor and
shattering into millions of dangerously sharp
pieces.

Trails of steam burst from cracks in the cavern,

filling the cave with an icy fog. I started to wonder if I was going to make it out alive at all.

Forcing myself to look at the queen, I saw that she was powering up.

This was it. This was the queen's finishing move for the human race.

She'd create a blast powerful enough to cut across the solar system. All of humanity would become enslaved if I didn't do something to stop her.

'Knock it off!' I shouted, trying to step forward but the force of the queen's power was pushing me back.

'It's too late, Chase!' the queen shouted. 'The storm is not coming! It is already here!'

The cavern was so cold that I couldn't generate a spark for another fireball. There was only one option left…

I'd have to tackle her.

The force of the queen's blast would eradicate *both* of us, but what choice did I have? The only way to save the planet was to sacrifice myself.

The queen arched her head back, focusing

her power directly over her head.

Stumbling forward, I realised I wasn't being held back by her invisible energy anymore. I mustered every ounce of strength I could and sprinted at the queen through the violently shaking cavern.

'*What are you doing?*' the queen shouted.

More chunks of ice fell to the floor, exploding before me as I ran across the cavern, gunning for the evil queen of Scrag.

'This one's for you, Earth!' I hollered.

As I jumped through the air, the ice volcano finally erupted. Huge pillars of ice broke through the floor of the cavern as the walls cracked.

My world turned white as I smashed into the queen. Intense pain flooded my body, but then it was gone...

Everything...was gone.

The human race was safe from enslavement by the queen of Scrag. I had done my duty as a ninja...as the defender of humankind, and the hero of—

'...cheeseburger,' a girl's voice said.

I shook my head. The voice had come from
my cousin, Zoe, who was seated on the bench
next to me. The rest of my friends were
hovering around the table, chuckling to
themselves.

'What?' I asked, confused.

Zoe smirked. 'I asked if you were feeling
okay. You didn't even touch your cheeseburger.'

'Yeah,' I said, wiping my mouth, hoping
there wasn't any drool. 'I'm fine.'

'It's just that I've been watching you for
about five minutes,' Zoe said. 'And I don't
think you've blinked once during that time.'

I scratched the back of my head. 'Um, I was
just thinking.'

Told you I wasn't really dreaming. I was *daydreaming*.

'I didn't say anything, did I?' I asked.

'Nope,' Gavin said. 'But every couple of seconds, your eyebrows twitched like you were *gonna* say something angry.'

I exhaled deeply, sitting up straight. 'What time is it? Is lunch over?'

'Yup,' Zoe said. 'Assembly's gonna start in a few. I wanted to grab you before it did since we're not sitting with the rest of the students.'

'We're not?' I said, scooping my book bag off the floor. 'Where are we sitting?'

'I'll be at the front of the gymnasium,' Zoe explained. 'You'll be nearby since you're my campaign manager.'

'That's right,' I said, shaking my head and returning to Earth.

Buchanan School was holding an emergency election to find a new president. The old president, Sebastian, was removed from office.

It's literally been three days since Sebastian was busted for trying to pull a fast one over the students and staff at Buchanan School. He lost his position as president, and Principal Davis felt like *that* was enough of a punishment so Sebastian was never suspended. He didn't even get detention!

All Sebastian had to do was issue an apology in the school newspaper. That was it! I guess kids with power barely get a slap on the wrist when they get in trouble.

Earlier in the morning, Principal Davis announced an emergency election at the end of the week, hoping to keep morale up. But looking at the students around the cafeteria, it seemed like no one really cared that there wasn't a school president.

It was Monday, and an assembly had been planned to take place after lunch that the entire sixth grade was attending. The candidates running for president were going to address the school. I wasn't sure who else was running yet, except for Zoe, who asked me to be her campaign manager.

Being the awesome cousin I am, I said yes. Or maybe I said yes because I was only half listening when she asked. I had just found some emerald ore in a video game, and I *had* to mine it! Can you blame me? *Do you know how hard it is to find emerald ore?* It's like finding a unicorn!

Anyway, that's how I became Zoe's campaign manager. No biggie though; I know it'd be awesome if she became school president. She'd actually be the first female president the school has ever had. You'd think after a hundred years,

Buchanan would've had at least *one* female president, but nope.

If you've kept up with my story, then you'll remember the skeevy note I got from the Scavengers last week. It said I had crossed a line and had awoken a sleeping giant, then it said that the storm was not coming, it was already here. That's probably why the queen of Scrag screamed it at me.

I only learned about the existence of the Scavengers a week ago when Naomi told me about the rumour. Naomi is a valued member of my ninja clan, but she's turned out to be a great friend too. I'm not sure what I would do without her.

Nobody knows who the Scavengers are or even if they existed for sure. Supposedly they're some kind of secret organisation within the school – so secret that people believe they're just a story to scare students.

I don't know though. I've been at Buchanan for a few months now, and I've never seen any evidence of them. But that doesn't mean they *don't* exist. Ninety-nine per cent of the kids at the school had no idea there were ninjas here either.

I expected to hear from the Scavengers again over the weekend, but I didn't. I even thought maybe they'd mess with me earlier in the morning, but they also didn't do that.

I was beginning to think that maybe Wyatt had sent the note. It sounded like something he'd do to just to get into my head.

Wyatt, in case you forgot, is the leader of the red ninja clan. He formed the new clan after his old clan kicked him out. The old clan appointed me as their new leader. Through some shady deals, Wyatt also became the vice president of Buchanan School. He even wore a homemade sash with 'VICE PRESIDENT' on it.

Thankfully, after Sebastian was fired, Wyatt wasn't allowed to take his place. Principal Davis suspected some foul play, but he couldn't completely prove anything. So he simply hit the 'reset' button on the whole shebang.

Oh, and in case you're wondering, I still have no clue who the white ninja is. A few weeks ago, the white ninja saved me from getting served a bowl of drop-kick soup by a bunch of Wyatt's red ninjas. And then saved me *again* during the talent show. I never found out who it was, and I haven't seen him since. Part of my brain is starting to think that the ghost of James Buchanan sent an angel in the form of a ninja to rescue me. But maybe not though – that's a bit farfetched, even for me...

I pulled my book bag over my shoulders and joined Zoe and my friends in the front lobby. Students were flowing through the halls, making their way to the gymnasium so they could find a seat for the assembly.

'Am I getting paid for this?' I asked Zoe.

'For being my manager?' Zoe said. 'No. It's a volunteer position.'

'But is it a *paid* volunteer position?'

Zoe stopped, folding her arms. 'Volunteer

means you don't get paid. Maybe you're the wrong guy for the job.'

'No!' I laughed. 'I'm kidding! I know what volunteer means, I'm just messing with you!'

'Really?' Zoe asked. 'Because this sounds like something you'd actually be confused about.'

'Really,' I said. 'And for the record, I'm happy to be part of this. You're gonna win this election so hard!'

'Right?' Faith said, clenching her fists in front of her. If her smile were a shining light, you'd be able to see it from space. 'This is all so exciting! When you're president, I want you to move the vending machines from the lower levels of school back into the cafeteria. I *hate* going into the Dungeon to get a bag of spicy fries!'

The Dungeon isn't deep enough to be considered a basement – it's probably about half a storey underground – but it's cold, dark and wet, so: the Dungeon. There also might be a dragon living down there. They say, late at night, you can hear the beast snoring …

'I'm not president yet,' Zoe said. 'But if I'm elected, I'll do my best to sort the vending machines out.'

'Whoa, whoa, whoa,' Gavin, Zoe's boyfriend, said. 'That's *after* you make sure they re-open the pool.'

'What pool?' I asked. 'We have a pool?'

'Yep,' Gavin said. 'Buchanan's got a bona fide Olympic-sized swimming pool that's been shut down for years.'

'Weird,' I said. 'It's probably a pretty dangerous place, right? And quiet too?'

My friends groaned, already knowing what joke I was about to make.

'Dangerous and quiet ... just like a ninja fart,' I said. 'Silent, but deadly.'

'There it is,' Zoe said, clapping her hands softly.

Everyone joined in clapping while staying stone-faced.

'It's funny!' I laughed.

'Keep telling yourself that,' Faith said. 'Maybe if you say it enough times, it'll *become* funny.'

Zoe looked at Brayden, who was walking at the end of our line. 'And what about you? Any special requests from you?'

'Not exactly,' Brayden smiled. 'I was going to keep this from you guys, but I've decided to run too.'

'Are you serious?' Faith asked.

I thought Zoe was going to get upset with Brayden, but she surprised me.

Her eyes lit up. 'That's cool! Are you going to introduce any monster-hunting classes if you get elected?'

Brayden is a self-proclaimed monster hunter. He swears there are werewolves running around the hills of our town, and he's devoted his life to finding one. He even runs a website where people can post their crazy monster theories to message boards. So far, there are only three members – Brayden, his mom and me…

'Actually,' Brayden said, 'I think I'm gonna go easy on the monster-hunter thing during my run. A lot of kids are afraid of what they don't know, and I'm pretty sure they don't know anything about monster hunting. If that little bit about me came out, I'd lose the election for sure.'

Faith chuckled. 'You hear that, Zoe? You can run a smear campaign against Brayden. That would make one less candidate for you to worry about.'

'I'm not running a smear campaign,' Zoe said. 'That's not the way I want to win. Besides, Brayden and I are friends. He wouldn't do that to me.' Zoe paused. 'Would you?'

'Never!' Brayden said. He stepped up to the gymnasium doors. 'See you guys on the flipside.'

After Brayden disappeared behind the gym doors, Gavin said, 'The flipside? Did we time travel back to the '80s?'

We all laughed.

Faith and Gavin said goodbye and headed down the hallway, to where the other students were entering the gym. Brayden had used the door that only the students running for office were allowed to use. And their campaign managers.

I held the door open for my cousin. 'Age before beauty.'

'I'm, like, a month older than you,' Zoe said. 'Are you calling yourself beautiful?'

'No,' I said, tripping over my words. 'I just … I mean … um …'

'Relax,' Zoe sighed, walking through the doorway. 'Don't hurt your brain. I need it in one piece.'

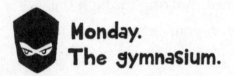 **Monday.**
The gymnasium.

Most of the students were already sitting in the bleachers, talking among themselves.

Zoe took the lead, walking down one end of the bleachers. 'As my campaign manager, do you know what your responsibilities are?'

'Yes,' I said confidently. 'But just in case, you should tell me anyway.'

Zoe sighed, frustrated. 'You're in charge of everything related to my campaign. Scheduling speeches, autograph signings, baby kissings, and so on.'

'You want me to set up a baby-kissin' booth?'
I joked.

'Creepy much?' Zoe replied. 'You need to be
the one who makes the posters and puts them
up all over school. You'll also be in charge of
encouraging kids to vote for me.'

'Isn't getting votes *your* job?'

'Yes, but you'll help. You can hand out "Vote
for Zoe" badges or something.' Zoe glanced at
me over her shoulder. 'You'll also need to figure
out how various groups of students feel about
me.'

'What do you mean?'

'Like, do the hipsters agree with my school
views? Are the jocks for or against me? Am I
doing well with the orchestra students? If not,
how can I win their votes? Those sorts of things.'

'Gotcha,' I said.

'I also need you to start thinking of some
great quotes for my acceptance speech, y'know,
if I *do* win,' Zoe said.

'Quotes?' I asked. 'How about something like,
"Dance like no one's watching"?'

Zoe's face scrunched up. 'Dude, I'm not talking to a bunch of cartoon princesses. These are *real* kids who have heard that quote a billion different ways. Gimme something better!'

I chewed my lip. 'How about, "Dance like *everyone's* watching"?'

Zoe slugged my shoulder, the same spot she hits every time! I bet my bone structure is starting to take a different shape from getting punched in the same place so often.

'Make it something about leadership,' Zoe snipped.

'Fine,' I said, rubbing my arm. 'I guess if I looked at myself, I'd like to think I was a good leader because I never cared about being better than the other guy. It's about always trying to be better than yourself.'

Zoe whistled as she scribbled in her notebook. 'That's a good one,' she said. 'I'm *so* using that.'

'Sure,' I said. 'It's not like I'll be using it.'

'And don't forget about tomorrow!' Zoe said.

I hesitated. 'What's tomorrow?'

Zoe's shoulders slumped as a worried look filled her eyes. 'Please tell me you're joking again.'

I tried to put up a poker face, but couldn't. 'You know I am, boss! Tomorrow's pizza party is all set. I've got fifty pizzas on deck for delivery during lunch tomorrow.'

Zoe's nose wrinkled as she smiled. 'Good.'

Want to know how awesome my cousin is? She's putting on a pizza party *buffet* for the entire sixth grade during lunch. And the best part? It's *totally* free for kids. All you have to do is show up, grab a plate and grab some 'za, which is what my dad calls pizza. She's calling it a 'free-za party', saying 'free-za' so it rhymes with pizza.

It's going to cost a lot of money, but Zoe is paying for the whole thing. Unlike me, she's been saving every penny of her allowance since she was five, waiting for the perfect thing to spend it on. I don't think she had to think twice about spending it on her campaign. And kids are going to go *nuts* about it too. This 'random act of awesome' might be all she needs to win the election.

From the corner of my eye, I saw a flash of light and then a *poomph*.

'Perfect!' said a boy's voice.

Zoe and I stopped to see who was talking to us. Briskly walking in our direction was a short kid, holding a giant camera that looked like it was from the 1930s, with the big metal bowl on top that held the flashbulb.

He was wearing dark brown khaki pants and a brown suit jacket and a brown tie. He was wearing a fedora with a slip of paper tucked into the strap that had the word 'PRESS' on it. He frowned as he approached.

'Now can I get one of the two of you together?' the boy said.

'Who're you?' I asked, stepping in front of Zoe so the kid couldn't take another photograph of her.

'Calm yourself, lad,' the boy said. 'I'm a reporter. I'm documenting the election for the school paper. The name's Melvin.'

MELVIN

'It's alright, Chase,' Zoe said, gently pushing me aside. 'Melvin's just doing his job.'

Melvin sighed. 'Trust me, I *wish* I were reporting a story that was more exciting, but my editor said I had to be here, so I am.'

'What's more exciting than an election?' Zoe asked, smiling like a movie star.

'*Ninjas*,' he replied without hesitating, zeroing his stare in on me.

'No such thing,' Zoe said immediately, sounding slightly nervous. 'At least at Buchanan. I mean, ninjas existed centuries ago in Japan, but that's it.'

I had to admit, Melvin had me kinda freaked.

'Ninjas? What're you talking about?' I asked, hoping I sounded genuine.

Melvin smacked his lips together. 'Lotta nasty rumours about a ninja runnin' around here. Plus there was that picture in the paper a couple of months ago. Hall monitors still ain't found the kid.'

Melvin was referring to an article in the school paper from a while back. There was a picture on the front page of a ninja stealing someone's stuff. The ninja was wearing black robes … *my* robes. In an effort to ruin my week, and maybe my life, Wyatt stole my ninja robes and ran around school, wreaking havoc on anyone and everyone. The school paper caught wind, snapped the photo, and claimed there was a ninja among us.

Most students have moved on from that rumour, but apparently *Melvin* had not.

'That photo was a fake, y'know,' I said. 'There aren't any ninjas in the school.'

Melvin's brow tightened. 'I took that photo,' he said coldly. 'I was *there*, man. I saw that ninja with my own two eyes.'

Zoe came to my rescue, changing the subject. She put her arm over my shoulder. 'Didn't you want a pic?'

Melvin lifted his humongous camera. 'Smile!'

Zoe smiled like a champ. I did my best to fake one. The bulb above Melvin's camera went off, making the *poomph* sound again as a ball of smoke appeared above it.

I rubbed my eyes. It was the brightest flash I'd ever seen in my life. I wouldn't be surprised if the front part of my brain was singed.

'Good luck with the election,' Melvin said as he walked past us.

'Weird kid,' I said.

'I know weirder,' Zoe smirked. 'You worried about the ninja thing?'

'Nah,' I said. 'We've gone this long without being discovered. We'll be fine.'

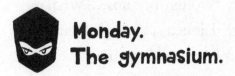 **Monday.
The gymnasium.**

Zoe was at the front of the gym next to Brayden. The other two candidates weren't with them yet.

Principal Davis stood in front of a podium, checking his watch and tapping his foot. Every few seconds, he would look up from his wrist and shake his head.

I was standing off to the side of the gym next to a set of bleachers. Naomi came over and stood with me.

'Excuse me!' came a voice from behind us. 'I'm running late!'

I was surprised to see a small girl with blonde hair jet past me. She was shorter than me, with very pale skin, but not gross pale – more like porcelain-doll pale. Cute too.

Naomi nudged my side with her elbow. 'Keep your eyes to yourself, tiger.'

I let out a snort through my nose. 'What're you talking about?' I joked, although I knew exactly what Naomi was talking about.

The girl ran past us and made her way to the area where the candidates were seated. She took the spot on the other side of Zoe, smiling and catching her breath.

Principal Davis nodded as he said something to her. She laughed and gave him a thumbs up.

Another voice came from behind Naomi and me, but this time it was gruff. 'Step aside, children.'

I turned around, not surprised to see Jake and his wolf pack.

Let me tell you a little bit about Jake. He's the cool kid in school. I'm sure there's someone at *your* school like him, just a different model number. Star quarterback, cheerleader girlfriend, and friends with a bunch of kids who are either good-looking or beefy jocks. The kids who tag along with Jake are known as his wolf pack.

I've been in Jake's crosshairs for a while, especially after last week's careers fair. Long story short – he chased me, and with some help from some good friends, I got away… but not before Jake got painted up like a circus clown for the whole school to laugh at.

I took a couple of steps back so Jake and his thugs could get through.

Jake glared at me as he passed, but I knew he wasn't going to try anything – not in a gymnasium full of students and teachers. That didn't stop him from shoulder checking me against the wall though. And in the same spot that Zoe had slugged me.

Thankfully that was it. Jake and his wolf pack climbed the bleachers until they were on the very top row, so they could heckle the students under them.

I looked back at the kids running for president. There was only one more empty seat at the front of the gym, which meant we were still waiting for one candidate.

All of a sudden, the gym lights shut off. Everyone gasped, but their surprise turned into shouts and cheers. It was a pretty typical reaction from a bunch of sixth graders.

Their shouts stopped when a crack of thunder shock-waved through the room. The sound had come from the speaker system.

A voice came through the speakers. 'Ladies and gentlemen, prepare yourselves for greatness! Your eyes will tear up at the sight of him! Your ears will pop at the wisdom that drips from his lips! Your hearts will melt at his dapper demeanour! Your brains will be blown from his philosophical school views! Guys and gals, please welcome the *next* president of Buchanan School, *Wyaaaaaaaaatt!*'

A spotlight lit up the centre of the basketball court, where Wyatt was standing with his arms in the air waving to the students in the bleachers.

He was sporting a smug grin, which just made the whole charade feel weird and creepy.

Then Wyatt stomped his foot on the floor, and the DJ to started playing techno music. As electronic music poured through the speakers, Wyatt spun in a circle and started *moonwalking* towards the podium.

I think the sixth graders were too shocked and confused to clap.

Wait, I take that back – *one* student was clapping wildly, the way a baby does when they first learn how to slap their hands together. It was Olivia Jones, Wyatt's girlfriend.

Wyatt continued his moonwalk across the gym, but it was obvious that he was getting tired. His smooth motions became jagged and robotic. I guess he shouldn't have started so far from the podium. Watching him was the most painful thirty seconds of my life. I kinda felt sorry for the kid.

At long last, he made it to the podium. The lights in the gym flickered back to life as he took a seat on the other side of the blonde girl. His chest was heaving up and down as he panted.

Principal Davis tapped on the mic. 'I'd like to thank everyone for skipping their classes for the last half of the day.'

The gymnasium of students chuckled quietly at his joke.

The principal continued. 'We're here today to meet the four students who are running for president. There's a camera in the back recording the assembly so the homeschooled kids in our district will be able to watch the speeches too. These students are also invited to cast their votes on Friday. After my short introduction, each of the candidates will make their speech. The speeches will be followed by a question and answer session. Don't hesitate to ask the tough questions here. They're expecting that. So please, if you will, give our candidates a round of applause!'

I whistled through my fingers as everyone clapped and cheered.

Principal Davis held his open hand out to each candidate as he introduced them. 'Give a hand to Wyatt, Daisy, Zoe and Brayden!'

Daisy was the girl's name, huh? It seemed to fit her.

The principal stepped away from the podium as he gestured to the four students running for president.

Wyatt was the first to step up to the podium. He flipped through a few index cards, squinting

his eyes like he was having a tough time reading his own handwriting. Finally, he tossed the cards over his head. With both hands, he gripped the sides of the podium and leaned into the microphone.

He paused for dramatic effect.

'I know I haven't been the greatest kid in the world,' he started.

Olivia shouted from the bleachers. 'It's alright, babe! We all deserve second chances!'

Wyatt smirked, pointing his finger at his girlfriend. 'Not all of us, sweetie. I know for a fact that a lot of students don't like me, and I don't blame them.'

Then Olivia stood, pumping her fist in the air, chanting, '*Wy-att, Wy-att, Wy-att!*'

Nobody joined in. Around the tenth time saying 'Wy-att', she fizzled out and sat back down.

Wyatt cleared his throat. 'I don't blame anyone if they feel anger towards me.'

I folded my arms. What was he trying to say?

38

'At the beginning of the year,' Wyatt went on, 'I tried to frame another student for stealing money from the food drive, and I've realised recently that I've never apologised.' Wyatt turned around with puppy dog eyes and looked at Zoe. 'So I'd like to start my speech... by saying I'm sorry. Truly I am.'

The crowd fell silent as they watched Zoe, waiting for her reaction.

Zoe give him a genuine smile. 'I appreciate that, Wyatt. I accept your apology.'

I knew my cousin would – she doesn't have a vengeful bone in her body, unless there's some kind of mysterious bone actually called 'vengeful'. I don't think there is, but don't take my word for it. I ain't a doctor.

Wyatt turned back to the crowd. After another dramatic pause, he said, 'There's a good number of kids who see me as the bad guy, with good reason. But I'm here to say that nobody ever sees *themselves* as the bad guy. Let me explain – do you think I walk the halls of our beautiful school with the intent of being evil? Do you think I wake up in the morning and wonder what kind of terror I could muster up for the day?'

'Yes,' I muttered quietly.

Naomi slowly exhaled, her eyes focused on the leader of the red ninja clan.

'I'm not the bad guy,' Wyatt said. 'I'm more like the *misunderstood* guy. Isn't everyone though? I'm a victim of labelling, and I'm here to tell you that labelling someone is just as bad as bullying someone. After enough time, the guy who's labelled will start *acting* like his label. Students, I'm standing here before you in our beautiful school to admit that I've messed up in the past. I know I don't deserve a second chance, but I'm asking you to give me one. I'm proof that kids can change, and a vote for me shows that we're all capable of change.'

I couldn't help but chuckle. Who did this kid think he was? What had he *changed* since the beginning of the year? It was the most ridiculous speech I'd ever heard, and I knew that the rest of the school wasn't going to fall for it.

As if the universe wanted to prove me wrong, the crowd of students cheered.

'Seriously?' I said aloud.

Wyatt wasn't finished. He pounded his fist on the podium and spoke loudly. 'And my first act, if elected president, will be to change our absurd mascot to something way cooler than a moose! We deserve better than that, and I'm going to make sure we get it!'

Everyone hollered again.

Yes, the moose was my idea. No, I wasn't proud of it. If I could take it back, I totally would, but the ball was already rolling when I realised everyone hated it. Like, *passionately* hated it.

Wyatt raised both hands in the air, holding up his index and middle fingers on each one, the universal signal for 'victory'. He moonwalked back to his chair with his arms up the whole time.

Next, Daisy took the stage. She cleared her

throat, but before I could hear any of her speech, someone tapped on my shoulder.

Mrs Robinson, my homeroom teacher, was standing behind me with her hand keeping the door to the gym open. 'I'm sorry to bother you,' she said, 'but you're needed in the front office.'

'Is something wrong?' I asked nervously.

'No, nothing like that,' Mrs Robinson said. 'There's a package for you.'

'A package?' Naomi said. 'Who gets a *package* at school?'

'Is it from my parents?' I asked.

'I have no idea. All it says is your name,' Mrs Robinson said tersely.

'How big is it?' I asked, hoping that maybe my parents had dropped off a next-gen console for me to unwrap. Hey, I can *hope*, can't I?

'*For the love of*—' my homeroom teacher grumbled. 'Just get to the front office and pick it up.'

Mrs Robinson pushed open the door and disappeared.

Naomi pointed to the candidates on the floor. 'What about Zoe? Don't you need to be here for her? You're her campaign manager.'

I glanced at Zoe, sitting in her chair, listening to Daisy's speech. Even though Naomi was right, what kid *couldn't* resist getting a package at school? I walked to the door and pushed the metal doorhandle down.

'It won't take long,' I said. 'Zoe doesn't need me during her speech. I'll be back before the question and answer session.'

'Oh no you don't,' Naomi said. 'You mean *we'll* be back, don't you?'

'Yes,' I said with a smile. 'That's exactly what I meant.'

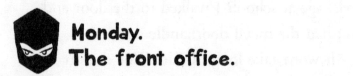

Monday.
The front office.

A few minutes later, Naomi and I were standing at the front office counter. Most of the staff were in the gym listening to the candidate speeches, but the nurse was still in the room.

'Can I help you?' Nurse Duvall asked.

'Mrs Robinson said there was a package for me?' I stated. 'The name's Cooper. *Chase* Cooper.'

'Been watching spy movies lately?' Naomi whispered, leaning back on the counter like she didn't care.

'*Maybe.*'

Nurse Duvall fumbled with something behind the counter. Then she set a small cardboard box in front of me. 'Here it is,' she said.

I studied the box for a moment. It was about the size of a thick textbook, which meant my parents did *not* drop off a next-gen console, even *after* all the hints I'd been dropping.

'Thanks,' I said to the nurse as I lifted it off the counter.

Nurse Duvall nodded and waved me out the door.

In the lobby, I held the box close to my ear and shook it.

'Is it heavy?' Naomi asked.

'Nope,' I said. 'I hear something in there, don't you?'

Naomi rolled her eyes. 'Duh. Pretty sure you wouldn't get an *empty* package.'

'What if it's a trap?' I asked.

'It's *not* a trap,' Naomi said.

'But what if it is?' I asked, nervous.

'It's *not*,' Naomi repeated. 'You think you're going to open that and a net's gonna fly out?'

I paused. 'What if it's an *ear*?'

'An *ear*? A *human ear*? What's the *matter* with you?'

'You're right. It's probably not an ear,' I said. 'But maybe … maybe it *is*.'

'Just open it already,' Naomi sighed.

I scraped my finger along the side of the small cardboard box, lifting the tape off the corner.

'Wait,' Naomi said. 'Now *I'm* worried this is a trap.'

'Too late!' I laughed, pulling the cover of the cardboard apart.

There was a moment where I felt the same thrill that I do on Christmas morning, but that thrill disappeared when I saw what was inside: a vulture mask that looked more cartoony than scary. After I touched the mask, I noticed there were actually *two* masks in the box.

Naomi paused, studying the masks. 'Sooo … that's not somethin' you see every day.'

I picked up the masks and checked to see if there was anything else in the box. There wasn't.

46

'Huh,' I grunted.

'Wait,' Naomi said, touching her finger to the bottom of the two masks in my hands. She lifted them slightly. 'There's something taped to the inside.'

When I flipped them over, I saw a fancy cream-coloured envelope. It was like the envelopes my parents got when a wedding invitation came in the mail. The envelope had 'YOU'RE INVITED' written on it in cursive.

I flipped it open and took out the thick card. The paper was smooth like velvet.

Naomi twitched when she saw it. I hadn't read the invitation, but I already knew who it was from.

INVITATION

THE HONOR OF YOUR PRESENCE IS REQUESTED AT THE CELEBRATION OF OUR NEWEST MEMBER, CHASE COOPER.

MONDAY, ONE-O-CLOCK IN THE AFTERNOON. ROOM 001 IN THE DUNGEON.

COOKIES AND DANCING TO FOLLOW.

THIS INVITATION IS FOR YOU PLUS ONE GUEST. ATTENDANCE IS COMPULSORY.

WE LOOK FORWARD TO SEEING YOU THERE. THE SCAVENGERS

CREEPY VULTURE MASK

The honour of your presence is requested
at the celebration of our newest member,
Chase Cooper.

Monday, one-o-clock in the afternoon.
Room 001, in the Dungeon.
Cookies and dancing to follow.

This invitation is for you plus one guest.
Attendance is compulsory.

We look forward to seeing you there.
The Scavengers

Naomi frowned, whispering, 'The Scavengers...'

I tried to lighten the mood. 'Seeing as how this is the *least* intimidating note I've ever received, I'm not too worried about it. I mean, *look* at the paper quality! It's even got a shimmer to it! I'm willing to bet this is 250gsm pearl white.'

'Wow,' Naomi said, raising her eyebrows. 'I have *no idea* what that means.'

'It means the Scavengers spent some money to make this invitation,' I said. 'I don't think a secret club would invest in something like this if they meant any harm.'

'Or, or, or,' Naomi said quickly and sarcastically, 'it means this secret club is so *delusional* and *dangerous* that they would declare war on someone in a fashionable way!'

I set the masks back in the box, and then pulled my pants up as if I were getting ready for some gruelling outdoor work.

'Well, then,' I said, doing my best 1800s farmer impression. 'We best not lolly-gag and see what all the fuss is about, seein' as how we were on the recievin' end of such a fanciful summons.'

'I'm not sure exactly what you just said, but it sounds like you're actually going into the Dungeon to meet with these... people.'

'The invite says I can bring a guest,' I said. 'Wanna be my plus one?'

'No,' Naomi replied. 'But since you're almost certainly not going to do the smart thing and stay away from there, I guess I'll *have* to accompany you.'

'Atta girl,' I joked.

Naomi slugged my shoulder. She's been working hard to perfect her one-inch-punch, and she was getting darn good at it.

'Ow!' I said. '*Why* does everyone keep hitting me there? It's like you guys all got together and agreed to keep jabbing the same spot over and over again until it falls off! That's something crazy monkeys would do! Is that why you're doing it? Did the crazy monkeys put you up to this?'

'Yes,' Naomi answered very seriously, as if it should've been obvious.

We headed for the Dungeon. Sure, it wasn't the smartest idea in the world, but deep down, I was excited at the thrill of something new.

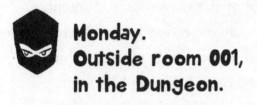

Monday.
Outside room 001,
in the Dungeon.

Since most of the students and staff were still
in the gymnasium listening to the speeches,
Naomi and I had no trouble walking down to
the lower level.

We stood outside room 001 and stared at the
humongous wooden door. Hanging over the
front of the door was a set of fake vines with
leaves that were gently rustling. A broken water
fountain directly behind us was pumping water
out of its tap.

'Do we knock?' Naomi asked.

'I guess,' I said, unsure. 'I hope there's not a secret phrase I need to know.'

'Considering you received an invite,' Naomi said, 'I'd bet they're expecting you.'

I held the vulture masks in front of me. 'Should we wear these or our ninja masks?'

Naomi stared at the masks for a moment. 'The Scavengers are expecting *you*, not a ninja. If we went there in our ninja outfits, I think the cat would be out of the bag.'

I shook my head. 'Who's putting cats in bags anyways? Seems like a mean thing to do.'

Naomi rolled her eyes.

I took a deep breath. 'Worst case scenario? We go in and they say a bunch of mean things to us, right?'

'Negative,' Naomi said. 'The worst case scenario is that you die.'

'Just me?' I asked. 'Not you too?'

'No way,' Naomi replied. 'Your death is going to be the distraction I'll use to escape. I'll be halfway to Tahiti before your funeral.'

I knocked on the wooden door three times.

From behind it, I heard several quick whispers and the shuffling of feet. And then the door opened a crack, revealing an eye. The eye darted back and forth between Naomi and me.

'Yes?'

I leaned closer, trying to get a better look at the kid behind the door, but the room was too dark. I held out my invitation. 'I got this just a few minutes ago. It said I was invited to something in this room.'

The door clunked shut.

'Well, that's that!' Naomi said. 'Can't say we didn't try! Let's get back to the gym. I bet Zoe's giving her speech by now.'

Another clunking noise came from the door. After that, it slowly slid open, but not more than a few centimetres. The kids on the other side weren't going to pull the door open for us. They expected us to enter at our own peril.

'Don't,' Naomi said. 'Seriously, this is messed up. Let's just leave now.'

I ignored Naomi's plea, pushing against the heavy door. It opened steadily. I tried to see what was inside, but the lights were out. It was dark, scary and dangerous – three good reasons to walk away, but you know how curious I can be.

The fake leaves spread as I stepped through, making a *shhhhhhh* sound. It was like walking into a secret area of a video game.

Naomi grunted as she followed me into the mysterious room. 'If we die, I'm gonna kill you.'

As soon as we were a couple of metres inside the dark room, the door slammed shut behind us. I spun around, but couldn't see a thing.

'Remember your training,' I said to Naomi.

'I could be wrong, but I don't remember any training that involved stepping into a trap,' Naomi said.

From the far side of the room, a voice spoke softly. 'Welcome, Chase. We've been expecting you.'

The long fluorescent bulbs flickered awake overhead, revealing a room full of kids wearing vulture masks. I was scared until I saw one of the kids standing next to the light switch by the front door. I don't know why, but when I imagined him flipping the lights on, I felt less afraid. I think it's like a magic act – when you understand the truth about what you were seeing, all the *magic* disappears.

I was simply standing in a room full of kids wearing the same dumb vulture masks.

The room looked completely ordinary. Desks were lined in rows just like all the other classrooms. Up the front, the whiteboard had some notes scribbled on it, which meant the room was still used for classes.

'Sup,' I said confidently. Holding up my invitation, I said, 'I got this in the front office. Is someone getting married down here?'

Naomi stood behind me. She stood a little taller when she realised I wasn't scared. At that moment, I felt like a strong leader.

One of the taller students stepped closer, but

THE SCAVENGERS

not too close. 'We've been watching you since the first week of school. You've been a strong blip on our radar that won't go away.'

'Well, I do go to school here, y'know,' I said sarcastically. 'Where am I gonna go?'

The boy ignored my remark. 'You've shown amazing potential, which is why you've received our invitation.'

I tossed the fancy cardstock onto one of the desks nearby. 'What's this about?'

'Isn't it obvi?' the boy asked, using animated gestures as he spoke. It was almost like our conversation was music that he was dancing to. 'This is because of your interference with Sebastian last week.'

'Sebastian?' Naomi said. 'What's he got to do with this? He's a Scavenger, isn't he?'

'Was,' the masked boy said. 'Sadly, he's no longer with us.'

I gasped. 'He's… *dead*?'

'*No, dude*,' the boy said, annoyed. 'I mean he's not a *Scavenger* anymore!'

'To be fair, you said that he wasn't "with us"

in a super creepy way,' I said. 'It sounded like he was dead.'

Everyone in the room stood silently, like mannequins.

'I've awoken a sleeping giant,' I said, repeating the words of the original note I received only a few days before. 'The storm is already here, right?'

'You misunderstand,' the boy said. 'The fact that we've revealed ourselves to you shows that we shouldn't be enemies. We should be working *together*. Never in the history of Buchanan has a Scavenger been taken down the way Sebastian was. You've shown true talent, and *that* is why you are with us today. You're the newest Scavenger. Congratulations.'

I looked at Naomi. She shook her head at me.

'May we offer you an orange soft drink?' the Scavenger asked. 'We know it's your favourite.'

'Um,' I said, a little confused. 'No thanks.'

The Scavenger pointed two fingers at Naomi. 'How about you? Naomi, right? You like tea, don't you? Earl Grey. Hot.'

Naomi chewed her lip. 'Yeah, it's my favourite, but…I think I'll pass.'

'Your loss,' the Scavenger sighed.

Across the room, another Scavenger holding our already prepared drinks sank his shoulders like he was bummed that we didn't want them.

Naomi stepped forward. 'What the heck are you guys? You've been nothing more than a rumour to the rest of the school, and now that I see you, I still don't understand why you guys even exist!'

Another one of the Scavengers stepped forward. She was shorter than the first, and had a very soft voice. 'We are the Scavengers, and we know everything about everyone. There are no secrets the Scavengers don't know. We are everywhere and nowhere.'

A voice started speaking across the room. 'Every conversation you've ever had has been listened to. Every note you've ever tossed in the rubbish has been collected and documented. Every student has a file with the Scavengers. Every. Single. Student.'

The girl in front spoke again. 'Your ninja clan might be a secret to the school, but not to *us*.'

I felt the air escape from my lungs. 'I guess the cat was never *in* the bag,' I wheezed to Naomi.

'We know everything about you, Chase,' the girl said. 'Your feud with Wyatt and his red ninja clan, with Jake, that Naomi and Brayden are members of your clan, your silly crush on Faith, your bee allergy, your mild intolerance to lactose ... we even know that your jaw sometimes clicks when you eat.'

I stared at the girl in the vulture mask, shocked. 'How is that possible?'

The Scavenger who first spoke when we entered the room crossed his arms. 'We told you. We know *everything* about *everyone*.'

'Oh yeah?' I asked, wanting to test them. 'If you know everything about everyone, tell me who the white ninja is.'

The boy paused. 'Of course we know who it is, but that information is just for Scavengers.'

'But why?' Naomi asked. 'Why bother with so much useless information?'

'*We* control this school,' the boy said. '*We* make the decisions around here. We've got the goods on everyone – staff, students, parents – and we know how to use that information to get what we want.'

'You guys can't know everything,' Naomi hissed. 'It's not even possible to—'

'You've been a member of Chase's ninja clan since the beginning, before it was even *his*. Wyatt recruited you because you bullied a student simply because he was in "your" seat during lunch. You embarrassed him so bad that he still avoids eye contact with you,' the girl Scavenger said plainly.

'Naomi,' I whispered. 'Is that true?'

Naomi stared at the floor. 'It's not something I'm proud of. It happened *before* you showed us what being a true ninja meant.' Naomi's eyes returned to the Scavenger. 'But that's information anyone would know – it happened in *front* of everyone. In front of—'

'You're jealous that Faith has caught Chase's eye because *you've* got a huge crush on him. For several weeks, you've been wondering if you should say something, but… How did you say it in your note to Zoe? You just "can't find the courage to tell him". Is that right? Zoe tossed the note into the rubbish bin in the girls' locker room. We simply… *collected* it.'

Naomi fell silent. Her face was expressionless as she stared at the floor.

I was speechless, not just at the fact that Naomi had a thing for me, but because the Scavengers really *did* know everything.

The leader of the Scavengers stepped forward, speaking with animated gestures again. 'Don't worry,' he said. 'Your secrets are safe with us, especially now that you're a member.'

'But I'm *not* a—' I started to say.

'We're excited to have you,' he said, talking over me. 'This might be a little quick, but there's no time to waste. Now that you're one of us, you'll have to quit your ninja clan. You can appoint a new leader if you want, but you can't say anything about your reason for leaving.'

I opened my mouth to speak again, but the boy was talking too quickly.

'After that, you'll take the presidency since *you* were the one who removed Sebastian from office. You'll run, along with the other candidates, but you'll win because *we'll* make sure of it.'

'But Zoe is running,' I said.

The boy paused, staring at me. 'So?'

'So no!' I said angrily. 'I'm not running against my cousin! I'm not quitting my ninja clan! And I'm sure as spew not joining your creepy little gang of rubbish pickers!'

The boy adjusted his vulture mask. 'I'm afraid the choice is not yours to make.'

Naomi was still staring at the ground. I felt awful for how embarrassed she must've felt.

'I make my own choices,' I said. 'And right now, I'm choosing to walk away from you. C'mon, Naomi.'

I turned around and started for the door. I heard Naomi shuffle her feet behind me.

'We won't stop you from leaving,' the Scavenger said loudly. 'But you can never get away from us. If you reject our offer, be prepared for a whirlwind of disaster coming your way. And don't even *think* about telling anyone about us, or it'll mean your *complete* and *utter* destruction.'

I glanced over my shoulder. All I saw were a bunch of kids wearing goofy bird masks. What kind of harm were they actually capable of?

Without saying another word, I left the room. The door shut as Naomi dragged her feet out behind me.

'Soooo,' I said, again trying to lighten the mood. 'Don't worry about all that in there, okay? I won't tell anyone that you've got a mega crush on the leader of your ninja clan.'

I expected Naomi to laugh, but she didn't. Instead, she ran down the hall, away from me. She didn't even respond to my comment.

'Slick, Chase,' I whispered aloud. 'Real slick.'

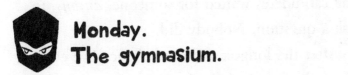# Monday.
The gymnasium.

After my meeting with the Scavengers, I went
back to the gym to watch the rest of the
speeches. Just outside the gym doors, I snapped
the two vulture masks in half and chucked
them into a rubbish bin — no need to carry
those ugly things around since I wasn't going to
play their game.

I caught the tail end of Brayden's speech,
which meant I completely missed Daisy and
Zoe's speeches.

Brayden was more confident than I expected
him to be, which was awesome. He promised

to increase the number of art and music classes, along with funding for more school trips throughout the year. The students responded pretty well. And not once did he mention werewolves, vampires or bigfoots.

The question and answer session started, and the candidates waited for someone, *anyone*, to ask a question. Nobody did.

After the longest awkward silence I've ever sat through, Principal Davis said everyone was allowed to hang out in the gym until school was out, and encouraged the candidates to mingle with the crowd.

Principal Davis wanted a new president in less than a week, and he thought doing an extreme 'meet and greet' session was necessary so students could really get to know who they were voting for.

'Chase!' Zoe said, running over to me. 'How'd you like my speech?'

I hesitated. 'I, uh, actually didn't hear any of it. I had to step out for a second, but I bet I would've loved it if I *was* here.'

'Thanks?' Zoe said, making it sound like a question. 'You should've been here. You're my campaign manager! What if I needed you during the speech?'

I wanted to argue, but I knew she was right. 'I'm sorry. It won't happen again.'

'Better not,' she joked.

Gavin joined us, taking Zoe's hand. 'Awesome speech!'

'Thanks!' Zoe said. 'You don't think I sounded shaky, do you? I was super nervous.'

'Not at all!' Gavin said. 'If you were nervous, you didn't show it. You were well spoken and very straightforward. Really, it was great.'

Zoe blushed.

I scanned the gym, looking for Naomi. The crowd of students was so thick that I couldn't see anything beyond a few metres. Most of the kids were clumped into groups around the other candidates. Even Zoe was attracting a horde of students.

'Can either of you see Naomi?' I asked my cousin and Gavin.

Gavin shook his head, standing on his tiptoes and gazing over the heads of the students.

'Not since before the assembly,' Zoe said. 'Is something wrong?'

I tightened my lips. Zoe knew Naomi had a crush on me, since it was *her* note the Scavengers took, but I couldn't say anything. 'No, nothing's wrong. I was just wondering where she went.'

At that moment, the speaker system crackled. There was a brief pause as the announcer fumbled with the microphone. Then a boy spoke. The same boy who had addressed Naomi and me in the dungeon.

'Attention, please! May I have your attention!' he said. 'Chase Cooper is currently struggling to fulfil his destiny! We encourage you to high five him every time you see him to give him the guts to continue. Don't forget to ask him about it too. Talking about it helps, Chase!'

My jaw dropped. What was that about? How did the Scavengers think *that* was going to encourage me to join their club?

The students who were gathered around Zoe started turning towards me. Then came the questions.

'Chase, what's up? What're you struggling with?'

'Yeah, man. Whatever it is, you know you can talk to me.'

'Go for it, man! Whatever that dude was talking about, you should just dive right in. Do it!'

'What kind of destiny are you supposed to fulfil? What were they talking about?'

'Tell us, Chase, what's going on? Seriously, if you need to cry, my shoulder's here for you, okay?'

Oh. That was the purpose of the announcement – unwanted attention. Way too much unwanted attention.

I tried telling everyone I had no idea what it was about, but that only fuelled their questions. Students pushed the issue harder, trying to get me to fess up to something I couldn't talk about.

'Chase, come on, man. Don't say it's nothing. What's up?'

'Bro, you can tell me! We're all sailing in this

ocean we call life. Now and then some of us find ourselves overboard. Bro, tell— bro, tell me— bro, look at me, bro. Let me throw you a rope.'

If the Scavengers wanted to put pressure on me, they were off to a good start.

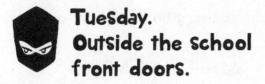 **Tuesday.
Outside the school
front doors.**

The next morning, I made it to school at a
decent time, *before* the first bell rang. I was
early enough that I had plenty of time to swing
by the cafeteria to get a breakfast sandwich and
a juice.

Kids were still asking me if something was
going on, but it wasn't as bad as it was after the
assembly. Most of the students would just point
at me in the hallway and say something nice,
which probably would've felt great if I knew it
wasn't because of a fake announcement.

71

As I was sitting at one of the tables, Zoe took the seat across from me. She was always early to school. *Always*. She was on the volleyball team, which had practice at seven in the a.m. *But wait, there's more!* Practice ended at eight, so Zoe joined the debate team to fill the rest of the morning before school started.

'Yo,' Zoe said, setting a bottle of juice on the table.

'Morning,' I said with a mouth full of sandwich.

'So are you going to tell me what that announcement was about yesterday or what?' Zoe said, spinning the cap off her drink.

I remembered the Scavengers' warning. I wasn't too keen on learning what they meant by my 'complete and utter destruction', so I decided to keep it from Zoe.

'No idea,' I said, taking another huge bite so I wouldn't have to talk anymore.

'Was it a prank?' Zoe asked. 'I bet Wyatt was behind it. Did you hear his speech yesterday?'

I nodded, pushing dry bread around my mouth.

'The nerve of him! Saying all that stuff about our moose mascot!' Zoe said.

'Don't you hate it as well?'

Zoe stuttered. 'Well, I mean, yeah, but *I* can say it. I'm your cousin, I'm supposed to give you a hard time. I don't really care.'

'A lot of kids do,' I said.

'Chase!' someone yelled from across the room.

I turned, expecting them to say something about another shoulder to cry on.

'Congrats, man!' the boy shouted, giving me a thumbs up.

'Glad to see you got your destiny figured out! Good luck!'

I stared, dumbfounded. What was going on?

He continued. 'Your posters are everywhere out here! You've got my vote for sure, good buddy!'

Zoe's eyes slowly met mine. 'Um, *what's* he talking about?'

My eye twitched. I didn't know for sure, but I had my suspicions. Terrible, *terrible* suspicions.

 **Tuesday.**
The lobby.

Zoe and I stared at the poster. Copies were plastered down the hall as far as the eye could see. On the huge poster was a photo of me. Someone had added the school flag waving in the background and an eagle soaring under me. The top of the poster said, 'CHASE COOPER FOR PRESIDENT. IF VOTING FOR CHASE IS WRONG, YOU DON'T WANT TO BE RIGHT.'

Zoe pushed her lips to the side. 'Sooooo, this is new.'

I said nothing. The Scavengers were behind

the posters; I had no doubt about that. If I said anything to Zoe, it could mean disaster for me, or worse, for her.

Zoe looked at me. 'What is this?'

I wanted to tell her everything, but I couldn't bring myself to do it. Fear makes you do stupid things sometimes.

'You could've told me you were gonna run, you know!' Zoe said. 'I would've been fine with it!'

Poomph!

'Perfect!' Melvin, the reporter, said. He was standing a short distance behind us, camera in hand, under a ball of smoke from the flashbulb. 'I think I really caught the anger in that one! Can I have another shot of you two fighting? After that, we can do a good handshake one. No, y'know what? Never mind. Let's get more fighting! Kids eat that up!'

'Get lost, Melvin,' Zoe growled. She turned back to me. 'And you! I feel like you stabbed me in the back!'

'But I…' I trailed off.

'But what?' Zoe said. 'You *what*?'

I sighed. Saying nothing only made me look *more* guilty.

Poomph!

'Nice,' Melvin whispered.

'Quit taking pictures!' I cried.

'You know you can't be my campaign manager anymore, right?' Zoe asked, raising her voice. She was clearly upset, and there was a crowd of students gathering around us. 'So now I'm left with no campaign manager and only *four* days until the election. I'm glad *you* got *your* posters out, but I'll be scrambling to catch up!'

My mouth opened slightly. 'Zoe, I...'

'Thanks,' Zoe said as she stormed off. 'Thanks for nothing!'

'Bummer,' said a student nearby. 'Don't let it get to you though. You've got my vote.'

'And mine,' said another student.

'Mine too!' yet another student said.

'And *my axe*!' some dude proclaimed from the back of the crowd. 'I'll be voting for you!'

In that moment, I felt really weird. I was torn. On the one hand, Zoe was upset with me. But on the other hand, several students just told me they'd vote for me. I was sad and flattered at the same time.

Daisy, one of the other presidential candidates, pushed through the crowd. She extended her hand to me.

'May the best kid win,' she said with a smile.

As I shook her hand, Melvin snapped another photograph. He was starting to get on my nerves.

'What made you decide to run?' Daisy asked, still shaking my hand like she was in a job interview.

'I just, uh...' I said. 'I dunno. I just wanted to?'

Daisy arched an eyebrow. 'Is that a question?'

I shook my head, trying to think of something better. 'I just thought the race could use a fifth student.'

'Ah,' Daisy said. 'Well, I'm glad to be running alongside you. Good luck.'

'Right,' I mumbled. 'You too.'

 **Tuesday.
Homeroom.**

I was the last in homeroom, on purpose I might add because Zoe was supposed to be there too.

Supposed to be.

I took my usual spot at the back of class. Zoe usually sat in front of me, but she wasn't there. It wasn't like her to be late for anything, which meant she probably wasn't going to come to homeroom at all. Being the super straight-A student she was, she was probably in the library.

Brayden was next to me. He leaned over and quietly said, 'I saw your posters. Pretty cool.'

I was surprised. 'You're not upset about it?'

'Not at all,' he replied. 'You're my best friend! Why would I be upset?'

I shrugged.

'Listen, man,' Brayden said. 'This whole week, we have to agree to not get upset with each other, alright? No matter what happens, this is just a stupid election, and it's not as important as our friendship, got it?'

I smiled and we bumped fists. I trusted Brayden, and I wanted to tell him that it wasn't my choice to run for president, and that it was the Scavengers who were messing with me, but I couldn't. Not yet at least. Brayden didn't even know the Scavengers exist, and that wasn't a bubble I wanted to burst.

Plus, the posters were just a prank to put more unwanted attention on me. There was no way my name was *actually* on the ballot. I was willing to bet if I just ignored the whole thing, everything would blow over. Basically I wasn't going to play the game with the Scavengers. My posters might be in the hallway, but that didn't mean I had to run.

Mrs Robinson stood from her desk and started with the announcements. 'First things first, I suppose. You all know the election for Buchanan's new president is going to be held this Friday, right *before* lunch. Votes will be counted *during* lunch, and the new president will be announced at the assembly *after* lunch. And…' Mrs Robinson paused dramatically. 'It looks like we have another student running. Chase Cooper?'

Not good.

Everyone in class turned to look at me. Don't you hate it when they do that?

Mrs Robinson's eyebrows lifted. 'Nice,' she said, and then droned on with the rest of the announcements. Her voice became a muffled trumpet as the room spun.

It looked like the Scavengers were playing for keeps. The posters with my ugly mug were hanging all over the school, and apparently they were legit. I *was* running for president now, whether I liked it or not.

 **Tuesday.
Art class.**

When I got to art class, I was happy to see Zoe in her seat. I wasn't planning on letting the Scavengers get the best of me, so I was going to withdraw from the election, but patching things up with Zoe came first.

I set my book bag on the floor and sat at next to hers. 'Look, about all the posters—' I started.

Zoe cut me off. 'S'cool,' she said, smiling softly. It was genuine, but there was still a hint of sadness to it. 'I was just shocked. That's all.'

'Really?' I asked. 'You don't hate me for it?'

Zoe shook her head, making an 'are you serious?' face. 'I'd never hate you for something like that. I might be disappointed, but just 'cause we won't be working together.'

'Don't worry about that,' I said without thinking. 'By the end of the day, things will be normal again.'

Zoe paused, confused. 'What do you mean by that?'

I shook my head, making some weird sounds that kind of sounded like I didn't know how to speak. High-pitched grunts mostly. I'd said too much, and my brain was starting to panic.

'This is about the announcement yesterday, isn't it?' Zoe asked.

Complete and utter destruction.

'It's nothing,' I said. 'I just meant that since you're not mad at me, we're good. Things are normal between us, right?'

Zoe nodded slowly. 'Riiiiiight.'

The rest of art went on as usual, which was lucky because Zoe is the best at giving someone the silent treatment. Our desks were literally a centimetre an inch away from each other, which would've made class super awkward.

As everyone else worked on their art projects, I was planning my next move with the Scavengers. I decided to pay them another visit right before lunch. That way, I wouldn't have to race the bell to get to any classes, plus Naomi could come.

I'd have to find her before that though – she was probably still embarrassed from the day before, but I wouldn't want to go into the Dungeon without her.

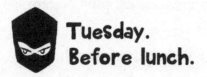 **Tuesday.
Before lunch.**

'Hi,' I said to Naomi when I saw her. I was by her locker, waiting for her.

'Hey,' Naomi said softly.

Yeah, she was definitely feeling uncomfortable.

'Look,' I said. 'Don't let yesterday make things weird between us.'

Naomi finally made eye contact. She looked angry. 'You think that's *all* that's bothering me?'

'Yeah,' I said, unsure. 'Until you said *that*.'

'I thought I knew everything there was to know about this school,' Naomi explained. 'There weren't any secrets that I didn't know about, and I was proud of it. I knew about our ninja clan. I knew about Wyatt's ninja clan. I knew about Glitch. I even knew about Suckerpunch!'

I felt more confused than ever. 'Glitch? Suckerpunch? Naomi, what the *heck* are you talking about?'

She ignored me. 'I knew all the rumours about the Scavengers, but I also knew there was *no way* they could exist without *me* knowing about them. And since I *didn't* know about them, they couldn't possibly exist, right?'

I stared at Naomi.

'Wrong!' she said. 'The Scavengers are real, and they're *terrifying*! They're worse than I thought! They know my secrets – *our* secrets, *everyone's* secrets! They know things they're not supposed to know! I want nothing to do with them, not now, not ever!'

'Mmmm,' I hummed. 'Then you're going hate me.'

Naomi stopped, her eyes piercing me. 'You're going down there again, aren't you?'

'I have no choice,' I said. 'You've seen my posters around the school, haven't you?'

She nodded.

'They've waged war on me,' I said. 'I need to meet with them. Hopefully I can talk some sense into their leader.'

'Do you know who their leader is?' Naomi asked.

I thought for a second. 'No, I have no idea. It's probably the tall kid who spoke the most.'

'I doubt they can be reasoned with,' Naomi said. 'I was there yesterday. They didn't seem interested in leaving you alone.'

I sighed. 'I know, but I have to try. Would you come with me?'

Naomi didn't answer.

I tried to be cute. 'Pleeeeeease? With strawberry syrup, whipped cream and cinnamon-glazed pecans on top?'

At that, Naomi laughed. 'What's with you and sweets? I bet your dentist makes millions off you.'

'Not me,' I joked. 'My *parents*.'

'Fine,' Naomi said. 'But under one condition.'

'Name it.'

'Never speak about my crush on you,' Naomi said. 'It was *months* ago. I'm totes over it now, got it?'

I had to force myself to keep a straight face. 'Got it.'

 **Tuesday.
The Dungeon.**

When Naomi and I reached the hallway of room 001, I stopped to get my thoughts together.

Naomi was in the middle of a sentence. '…which is why I feel like the Scavengers are kind of like the ninjas to actual ninjas. Y'know what I mean? Like, they were so secret that not even a ninja clan knew about them! While ninjas live in the shadows, the Scavengers live in the *ninjas'* shadow. Messed up, right?'

I watched the hallway for any movement, making sure we were alone. I didn't want to admit it, but I was scared. I could tell Naomi was trying to lighten the mood.

'Chase?' Naomi said, stepping in front of me. 'Earth to Chase. You're needed back on Earth, sir. Hey, here's one – if a ninja falls in the forest, and nobody is around to hear it, did the ninja make a sound?'

Smiling, I answered. 'For starters, ninjas *don't* fall. For, um, *seconders*, the ninja wouldn't make a sound anyway – he's a *ninja*. And thirdly, just trust me on it, if the ninja *did* make a sound then he was *never* a ninja to begin with.'

'Take *that*, imaginary ninja who fell in the forest,' Naomi said. 'Burn, sucka!'

Putting my game face on, I said, 'I'm just going to tell them to knock it off.'

'Because that worked yesterday,' Naomi said sarcastically.

'I'll just say I'll go straight the principal if they don't quit.'

Naomi made a 'duh' face. 'You probably should've done that first.'

'You might be right, but I'm afraid I'll just

make things worse if I do that first. I just want to give them a chance to do the right thing.'

'Some kids don't *want* to do the right thing,' Naomi said. 'Some kids just want to play dumb games. You heard them yesterday; they control the school. What makes you think they'll stop playing *that* game?'

'You're not helping,' I said, marching towards room 001.

Naomi followed me, continuing her case. 'Seriously, I don't think this is something you should even flirt with anymore. These kids are hardcore.'

'So I should just ignore it? Pretend it's not happening?' I asked, stopping in front of the spot we stopped at the day before. The broken water fountain behind us was still pumping water through its tap.

'No,' Naomi said. 'I don't know the answer to that.'

'Exactly,' I said. 'So I'm going to try this first. I promise, if it doesn't work, I'll do it your way.'

I turned and reached for the doorhandle...

But the door wasn't there. Neither were the fake vines.

'Ummm,' I hummed, glancing down both sides of the hall. 'Isn't this where we were yesterday?'

'There's the busted water fountain,' Naomi said, pointing. 'And down there is room 002.'

Where a door should've been was a massive brick wall with a street sign for 'Brackenbury Lane' and an arrow pointing left on it.

'What the?' I asked, confused.

Naomi knocked on the bricks to check if they were fake, but they weren't. 'If there was ever a time to freak out, it would be now,' she said, rubbing her sore knuckles.

I reached out to knock on the wall, but Naomi stopped me.

'It's solid,' she said, waving the pain out of her hand. 'I wouldn't bother.'

I sighed, but listened. It wasn't necessary to bang on the bricks if it was just going to hurt my hand. I *need* my hands!

A rustling came from down the hall, and then a small voice said, 'You guys okay?'

It was Daisy.

I pointed at the brick wall where room 001 was supposed to be. 'There should be a door here, right? Are we crazy?'

Daisy stepped up to the bricks, running her fingers down the wall. She squinted thoughtfully. 'I'm not sure,' she said. 'If there was, I never had class in it. But now that you say it... I *think* I remember a door being here. Weird.' She turned around and said brightly, 'So how's the race going?'

'It's going,' I replied.

'What'd you think of my speech yesterday?' Daisy asked, obviously fishing for compliments.

I decided that honesty was best. 'I missed it. I had to leave the gym for a few minutes.'

'Oh,' Daisy said sadly. 'Oh well. It's not like I would've won your vote since you're running.' She turned and headed towards the stairs that led to the ground floor. 'See ya upstairs.'

'See ya,' Naomi mumbled, returning her attention to the magical brick wall.

Room 001 wasn't there anymore, even though Naomi and I had *just* been inside it the day before. There was no way someone could've built a *brick wall* in less than a day!

A chill travelled down my spine, shooting into my legs until my toes tickled.

'Let's get out of here,' I said, looking over my shoulder. 'This is too weird, even for *me*.'

Naomi nodded, and together, we went back upstairs. Lunch had just started, and being around a whole bunch of kids sounded better than standing in a cold dungeon.

 **Tuesday.
The lobby.**

I was still trying to wrap my head around how room 001 could've disappeared when Naomi and I entered the lobby.

'It's not possible,' Naomi said. 'That door *has* to be there. It just *has* to. I bet it was behind those bricks.'

'Yeah, but being down there gave me the creeps…' I stopped, watching the *huge* line of students waiting to get into the cafeteria. 'What's going on?'

Naomi peered through the tinted glass windows into the lunchroom. 'Oh, it looks like a pizza party!'

I slapped my forehead. 'That's right! Zoe's party is—'

Before I could finish my sentence, Zoe screamed at me, '*How could you?*'

I turned around and saw Zoe storming across the lobby, looking furious. Her eyes were red with fire, and her cheeks were wet with…tears?

'What are you—'

Again, Zoe cut me off, but not with words. She slapped me with her open hand.

Naomi froze, her eyes wide.

The sound echoed across the lobby, and maybe even across the state. I bet somewhere a flock of birds got scared out of a tree because of that slap. Everyone waiting in line flinched at the same time when they saw it.

'*Oh snap!*'

'*I think you mean, oh SLAP!*'

'*Dang! That girl can hit!*'

'*Owned!*'

I rubbed my cheek. '*What gives? Are you crazy?*'

'That pizza party was for *my* campaign!

I paid for it! What else of mine are you gonna steal?' Zoe screamed.

'What are you talking about? I *just* got here!' I replied, but I quickly saw what Zoe was talking about.

Through the tinted glasses windows, I saw a banner with my face on it. I took a step closer to the window, still rubbing my burning cheek. And then I read the banner aloud, 'Have a slice on me, Chase Cooper. A vote for me means free pizza for you…'

Poomph!

I was beginning to hate the sound of Melvin's camera.

'Zoe, I didn't do this,' I said, but when I turned around she was gone. I suddenly felt so mad that Zoe had slapped me in front of everyone and just disappeared a second later.

'Fine!' I shouted loud enough that she could hear me wherever she was. 'Then you can't use my awesome leadership quote!'

I know. I regretted it the second I said it, but everyone was staring at me. I had to save face, right?

Naomi pursed her lips, but didn't say anything. She looked at me, and then down the hallway to where Zoe had run off.

I took off running, but I'd barely made it a few steps before a tall boy got in my way. With his chest pushed out, he bumped into me. I staggered a bit, but managed to stay standing.

'Move!' I ordered.

The boy refused, smirking the entire time. He raised his hand, showing me an index card with writing on it. 'Read it,' he said.

I stared at the card, confused. 'Huh?'

'Read it,' the boy said, 'or we'll tell everyone you're a ninja.'

Grinding my teeth, I looked at the card again. If all I had to do was read a sentence to avoid having my secret exposed, then fine. I read aloud. 'My name is Chase Cooper, and I approve this message.'

The smirk never left the boy's face.

'What's this about?' I asked.

The boy ignored my question and quietly said, 'We are everywhere…'

'And nowhere,' a girl said, stepping up to his side.

'Everything you believe to be secret…'

'…is not. We know everything about everyone.'

Scavengers. And they were finishing each other's sentence, which was even creepier than you'd think. Naomi stood next to me, opposite the girl. I looked for Melvin, but he wasn't around anymore. The line of students waiting for pizza was moving quickly enough that nobody was paying attention to us.

The boy narrowed his eyes. 'You've offended us, and now you must pay.'

I put my hands out in front of me, ready to block any punches that were thrown.

The girl giggled. 'Not with a fight,' she said. 'We will destroy you for rejecting our invitation, but not with bruises or black eyes...'

'It's your *legacy* we're after,' the boy said.

After that, both of the Scavengers disappeared through the cafeteria doors.

As if on cue, Wyatt and Olivia stepped *out* of the lunchroom.

'Jeez, really?' Naomi whispered to me. 'It's like your enemies are lining up to take shots at you.'

I imagined a conference room filled with all the kids who have tried messing with me over the past few months. They were seated at a huge mahogany table, sharing stories of how they *almost* got me 'that one time'. They'd probably have a sign made for the name of their evil league, something like 'Chase-Haters

Club'. There'd be a yearly fee of ninety-nine bucks that had to be—

Y'know what? Let's get back to the story…

His mouth wet with pizza grease, Wyatt held up a paper plate with *three* fat slices of pepperoni pizza on it. 'Nice move with the pizza,' he said. 'But it won't win you the election.'

Olivia had her own plate with several slices of pizza stacked on top of each other. 'My boo's got this election in the palm of his hand! He's only a few points behind you, but by the end of the week, he'll be in the lead.'

'A few points behind me?' I asked. 'How do you know how many points anyone has?'

'Student surveys,' Melvin said as he walked towards us. He had his own plate of pizza. 'You're in the lead right now, Chase.'

'I am?' I asked, not surprised since everyone thought I had given them free pizza.

'Daisy's second, Zoe's third, Brayden's fourth, and Wyatt?' Melvin said, glancing at the leader of the red ninjas. 'You're last.'

'So much for being a few points behind me,' I said.

Wyatt tore a chunk of pizza off into his mouth. 'We'll see what place you're in by the end of the week.'

'How's *Daisy* in second place?' Olivia asked.

'Homeschooled kids,' Melvin said. 'Seems most of them are on her side.'

'Homeschooled kids shouldn't count!' Wyatt huffed. 'They're not students here!'

'They count,' Melvin said flatly. 'One of my best friends is homeschooled and lives in the Buchanan district. I'm glad he's got a vote if it means you've got less of a chance of becoming president.'

Wyatt let out a *pfft* as he made an ugly face, but he didn't say another word.

Olivia stuck out her tongue as the creepy couple went back into the lunchroom to stuff their faces with more greasy pizza.

Naomi said goodbye and then stood in line behind the other students waiting for lunch.

It was just Melvin and me in the lobby now.

The reporter sighed, holding his oversized camera in front of him. 'Looks like you're the kid to follow around, right?'

'Because I'm winning?'

'Nope,' Melvin said. 'I got a text message from an unknown number telling me I should tag along with you at all times.'

'Why?'

Melvin paused. 'It said you know something about the ninjas.'

I choked, coughing loudly.

Putting his hand on my shoulder, Melvin said, 'You alright? Need some water?'

Hacking violently, I put my hand to my mouth, shaking my head.

'Between you and me?' Melvin started. 'I *know* there are ninjas hiding in the school. In fact, do you remember that ninja act in the talent show a couple of weeks back?'

'Yeah,' I said, avoiding eye contact.

'Well, I believe that *wasn't* an act,' Melvin said. 'I think those ninjas were in the middle of a fight that just happened to land in front of an audience. If I can bring this story out into the light of day, you know how much attention it would get? It'd be the biggest news to hit Buchanan since the chocolate milk disaster of 2010.'

'The what?'

'Students are limited to two chocolate milks during lunch for a reason. Back in 2010, the limit was lifted and students were allowed to drink as much as they could afford,' Melvin explained. 'Kids were barfing chocolate milk in record numbers. You know how some kids give no warning that they're going to puke? Instead, they just pop at their desk? Just think of the whole school doing that. All. Day. Long.'

I gagged. 'Can you imagine the smell?'

'I'd rather not,' Melvin said. 'This ninja story is going to blow that one out of the water. I'll be the most famous reporter in the world.'

There was no doubt in my mind that it was the Scavengers who sent Melvin the text. If Melvin trailed me long enough, he was sure to find out about my secret ninja clan.

Running for president. Damaging my friendship with Zoe. Making things awkward between Naomi and me. Telling Melvin that I knew anything about the ninjas. All that, and it was only Tuesday!

I didn't even want to *think* about what else could possibly go wrong, because the truth was I knew things could be worse ... I just didn't realise how much worse.

 **Wednesday.
Homeroom.**

When I got to school the next morning, I had
a sick feeling in the pit of my stomach, like
something terrible was waiting for me as soon
as I stepped through the doors. I was surprised
to see that it was just the opposite.

Normally I can make it to homeroom
without a single person noticing me. My run
for president changed that.

'*Chaaaaaaaase!*' said a boy wearing circle
sunglasses as he pointed at me with both his
hands.

A girl smiled at me, touching my shoulder as

she walked by me in the hallway. 'Awesome pizza party yesterday! Me and all my friends are *totes* voting for you!'

Someone shouted from down the hall, 'Chase Cooper! The Coopster for president!'

Everyone in the corridor cheered.

And to be completely honest – I didn't *hate* all the attention I was getting.

For those first few comments, I tried to maintain an air of integrity, keeping my head high while weaving through the crowd. But soon the crowd grew thicker, and it was impossible for me to even move because of the wall of students around me. I couldn't help but smile.

'Chase, can I get your autograph?' asked a girl, holding her diary out for me to see. The book was opened to a page where she drew a heart around my name.

Another boy pushed forward. 'Dude, street hockey tonight! My street! Everyone who's cool is gonna be there! No need to bring skates 'cause we've got a pair for you!'

Someone else held a baby doll to my face. 'Kiss my baby, Chase!'

'Guys, guys, guys!' I said, patting at the air in front of me. I was going to be serious, but my ego got the best of me. Can you blame me? 'Easy on the Coopster! There's plenty of me to go around!'

Everyone laughed.

 **Wednesday.
Homeroom.**

I spent so much time joking with my new fans
in the hallway that I didn't even hear the
second bell ring. Principal Davis had to break
the crowd up, but nobody was in trouble. He
always threatens detention but never delivers.

Mrs Robinson was already in the middle of
the morning announcements when I entered
the room. A couple of boys nodded at me
when I walked in. A few girls fluttered their
eyelashes in my direction.

Being popular was something I could get
used to.

'Sup, King Tut?' I said, sitting in the desk behind Zoe. Maybe throwing out random nicknames was a little bigheaded of me.

She didn't answer.

I leaned forward in my chair. 'Hello?'

Again, Zoe said nothing. She was still mad, and she was showing me by giving me the silent treatment. Even after my awesome morning, I still felt bad that she was upset. And she had every right to be! The pizza party that was supposed to be hers was hijacked by the Scavengers, turning it into mine!

'Zoe,' I whispered. 'I'm sorry about yesterday.'

'Then why did you do it?' Zoe replied swiftly.

For a split second, I thought about unloading about the Scavengers and their role in how my week was turning out, but again, I decided to keep it to myself. There wasn't any reason to involve her yet since the fire was still burning.

'I can't tell you what's going on,' I said, 'but I'm going to fix this. I promise.'

Zoe folded her arms. I watched the back of her head as she replied. 'This isn't something you can fix, Chase. You've done too much damage this time.'

'But…' I said, trailing off. I didn't know what else to say.

For the rest of homeroom, I sat quietly trying to figure out what my next move against the Scavengers was going to be. If I let it go on for too much longer, I was going to lose Zoe as a friend, and her friendship meant more to me than anything.

 **Wednesday. Lunch.**

The rest of the morning proved to be awkward since I have several classes with Zoe. The silent treatment she was giving me was like an invisible wall separating us. It was even worse because in *all* of our classes, our seats were right next to each other. Her refusal to even *look* at me was driving me crazy.

During lunch, I was able to take my mind off her for at least a few minutes after I sat at a table alone with my food.

Just then, Jake slammed his tray on the table and sat across from me. His wolf pack remained standing, scouring the room with beady eyes.

'Where's Melvin?' Jake asked.

I grunted. 'Huh? The reporter?'

Jake pushed his tongue around like he was trying to get food out of his teeth. 'Yes, the *reporter*.'

'Why?'

'Because I'm *looking* for him,' Jake answered, irritated.

'I don't know,' I replied. 'I haven't seen him today. What do you need him for?'

Jake smacked his lips, and then spit a tiny piece of food onto the floor. Standing from the table, he said, 'If you see him, don't tell him I'm looking for him. In fact, if you see him, come find me.'

'What makes you think I'm gonna do that?' I asked.

Jake looked me dead in the eye. 'Because we both want him to keep his mouth shut about ninjas.'

Great. More drama for me to swim around in.

I'd hardly touched my food. I was too busy watching everyone in the lunchroom. Naomi was eating with some of her friends. Zoe was making the rounds from table to table, talking politics and trying to win votes. Daisy, Brayden and Wyatt were doing the same thing. If I were actually running for president, I'd probably be doing it too.

Right then, I heard Melvin's voice. 'I *knew* following you was the right thing to do! Felt it in my gut!'

Slowly, I looked all around me, but couldn't see Melvin anywhere. 'Um,' I said. 'Where are you?'

'Down here!' Melvin whispered from *under* the table.

'Okaaaay?' I said, not making any sudden movements. And then I realised he had heard my conversation with Jake.

'Tell me what you know about the ninjas!' Melvin ordered, still whispering as he pressed a pencil against the paper of a small notebook.

'Dude-man,' I said. 'Get outta there.'

'Tell me what I want to know!' Melvin said. '*Why* did Jake confront you about ninjas? *What* do you know about them?'

I kicked at Melvin, not hard, just enough to annoy him, like he was a bug I was trying to shoo away. 'Get out of there!'

Melvin scooted out from under the table. The back of his shirt was caked in crumbs and dried bits of food. Gross.

'What'll it take for you to talk?' Melvin asked. 'Huh? Name it! Anything! I swear I won't mention your name in the article.'

'Get lost,' I said. 'Jake's looking for you, and if you stand around here for too long, he'll *find* you. And you definitely don't want that.'

Melvin looked over his shoulder, tapping his

pencil on his notepad. 'There's a story here,' he said. 'And I can either take it from you or you can give it to me.'

I paused, acting like I was going to say something important. 'Alright, this one time…' I started.

'Mmm?' Melvin hummed with a smile, scratching words into his notebook.

'I thought I found a human finger half buried in the dirt out on the track,' I said. 'But it turned out to be just a dried up hot dog.'

Melvin's pencil stopped. 'Funny,' he said sarcastically.

'Seriously!' I said. 'Sounds like a happy ending, but where'd the hot dog come from, Melvin? Huh? *Where did the hot dog come from?*'

'So immature,' Melvin said with a drop of disgust in his voice.

'Me? Immature?' I asked. 'I collect comic books because they're going to be worth something someday, okay? I'm investing in my future! Does that sound like something an immature person would do?'

Melvin shook his head, disappointed that I wasn't helping him with his ninja story.

I sighed, turning back to my food. 'Whatever, dude. Just leave me alone.'

Melvin hesitated like he was going to say something, but he didn't. Suddenly he spun around and jogged towards the cafeteria doors.

'C'mon,' I heard Jake's voice say from nearby. 'He saw us.'

I gritted my teeth. Jake had spotted Melvin. I couldn't just sit by, knowing that Jake was planning on giving the reporter the beat down of the century.

Jake was storming down the aisle. I grabbed my tray of food and jumped up just as he crossed my path.

The leader of the wolf pack slammed into me. I could've kept my balance, but I needed to make a scene if Jake was going to be stopped.

Flipping my tray towards me, I splashed all the nasty cafeteria food all over my face and hair. Sloppy joe and banana cream pie are *not* two items I'd recommend going up your nose.

'Dude!' I shouted, acting shocked.

The students in the cafeteria snapped their attention towards us like squirrels when they hear twigs snap.

Jake took a step back with his arms out, looking down at the mess of food on his shirt. *'Are you serious?'*

I stole a glance behind me to see if Melvin was still around. He wasn't, which meant he was safe … for now.

I started acting upset so Jake would waste more time arguing with me instead of searching for Melvin. Pointing at my crushed apple on the floor, I said, 'No, are *you* serious? You killed my apple, dude! You think those things just grow on trees?'

Jake started to argue, but his face froze. I could almost see his brain crashing. 'Uh…yeah?'

I threw my arms up. 'Oh right, like there's some kind of *magical* tree out there that grows apples! Some sort of mystical all-powerful tree that some wizard created *just* to show his big brother that he was all grown up now, right?'

Jake's eye's narrowed in confusion. 'What are you talking about?'

'Sorry,' I said, wiping greasy beef off my face. 'I just really wanted that apple.'

Jake took one step towards me and growled. 'I know you did that to keep Melvin safe, but you can't be there all the time. I will find him, and I will keep him from writing that article.'

I acted clueless. 'What? Was Melvin around? Where?'

Jake's jaw muscles twitched, but the conversation ended there. He raised his fist, the signal for his wolf pack to follow him. Like mindless animals, they trailed behind him as he returned to one of the lunch tables.

Wiping the rest of the slop off my face, I took a knee and started scooping food back onto my tray. After all the junk I'd been through in the week, I felt a little better at having helped Melvin avoid a black eye or two.

That moment only lasted for a second though.

The lights in the cafeteria dimmed. Hushed whispers floated through the crowd.

At the front of the cafeteria, the stage curtains swept open, revealing a giant LCD television. An image of Buchanan School slowly came to life onscreen as the audio played through the cafeteria speaker system.

'Buchanan School...' said the narrator. 'A place of peace, hope and love. A place where friendships are forged in the fires of life. A place where education is the highest priority... right after pizza parties.'

The kids in the lunchroom laughed simultaneously.

The video went on, filtering through photos of students in class. 'But there is another threat to our wellbeing...'

I gazed at the television, hypnotised.

The image on the screen turned bright red as Brayden's class photo spun to a stop at the centre. 'This boy, who you know as Brayden, has a dark secret.'

Gulping, I quickly scanned the room looking for my best friend. I found him standing at the far corner of the cafeteria. His brow was furrowed, and his lips were tightly pressed against his teeth as he watched the video.

'Brayden is a self-proclaimed werewolf hunter,' the narrator said calmly. 'He's devoted most of his life to finding and capturing a real-life werewolf, which any sane person would tell you don't exist. Brayden is chasing ghost stories.'

The screen flashed white and a *DUN* sound effect cut through the cafeteria. There was another photo of Brayden on the screen – a much more embarrassing photo of him in his werewolf hunting armour.

'Is *this* the student you want running the school?' the narrator asked.

Holy wow. Who on earth had the guts to play a commercial like that in front of the entire school? Who would even sink to the level of making a smear campaign video?

Brayden's red photo faded out on the screen, only to be replaced by a bright and shiny photo of…

Me.

The narrator continued. 'A vote for Chase Cooper means a vote for reality. Chase lives in the *real* world, with *real* kids, and has *real* goals. A vote for Chase Cooper means no time wasted on the pursuit of fake monsters. A vote for Chase Cooper…is a vote for the future.'

The commercial faded to black, and my voice came through the speaker system. '*My name is Chase Cooper, and I approve this message.*'

I bit my tongue. The Scavenger recorded me when I read that stupid index card! Why did I even read that thing? Why can't my brain put these things together *before* bad things happen?

Principal Davis jumped onto the stage and shut the television off, but it was too late.

The cafeteria lights came back on, but the students remained mostly quiet. More whispers came from the crowd, but the conversation wasn't about me. It was about Brayden.

When I turned to look, he was glaring at me, fuming. He was so angry that I could see the muscles twitching in his jaw. I've never seen him so upset.

Principal Davis strode over to me. 'Chase,' he said, obviously furious. 'A word in the hallway, please.'

I was thankful to have a reason to leave.

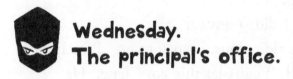

Wednesday.
The principal's office.

'At what point did you think it was okay to make a video like that?' Principal Davis asked loudly, sitting behind his desk with his arms folded.

I didn't answer.

'Do you know the world of trouble you've put Brayden in? Aren't the two of you best friends?'

I nodded.

'Did it never occur to you that playing a smear video like that would hurt your friendship?'

Again, I didn't answer.

'This is ridiculous, even for you,' Principal Davis said. 'I can't let this go, Chase.' He sighed, slumping down into his leather chair. Leaning back, he folded his hands on his stomach. After a moment, he spoke again. 'When you put your name in for president, I was excited. You've been a great addition to this school since day one. You've been nothing but a force of good and an outstanding role model...'

Every word hurt. I wanted to cry out and say that I was still those things and that it was the Scavengers who were tarnishing my reputation, but I couldn't bring myself to do it.

'I want to believe there's more to the story than a simple video,' Principal Davis said. 'Do you have anything to say for yourself?'

'No,' I said softly.

Principal Davis nodded as he delivered my punishment. 'Detention for the rest of the day. All-day detention tomorrow, but you'll serve it by cleaning the school grounds – community service. And on Friday, you'll be on the clean-up crew after breakfast in the cafeteria.'

'Okay,' I said.

Scribbling on a pad of paper, Principal Davis filled out paperwork that would probably get filed away in my permanent record. I sat patiently, watching the hands on his clock.

All week I had been trying to figure out how to get out of the way of the Scavengers' path of destruction, and Principal Davis just did it for me by basically putting me behind bars until the election on Friday.

I exhaled slowly, sinking down in my seat. If I had to sit in detention for a day and half, I could just coast through the rest of the week on cruise control. Honestly, I was kind of looking forward to it.

Have you ever heard of someone so excited to rot away in detention? Yeah, me neither.

 **Wednesday. Detention.**

Mr Lien was resting his head on his hand when I got to detention. Mr Lien was the unlucky staff member who was closest to the detention room, making him the most convenient choice to supervise detention.

And you could tell he hated it.

With his eyes half shut, he mumbled, pointing to a sheet of paper at the edge of his desk, 'Name and grade.'

I snatched the pen and signed my name. I took the desk at the end of the row, furthest from the door.

'I'll be back and forth between this room and my class across the hall,' Mr Lien said. 'You need anything, just shout out. Understood?'

'Yes sir,' I said.

Mr Lien pushed himself away from his desk and waddled out of the room.

Finally alone, I dropped my book bag onto the floor and rolled my head around in large circles, stretching my muscles out so I could relax.

The last time I was in detention, time seemed to stop. Every second felt like an hour, and every hour felt like an eternity. I remember being so bored I felt like I was going to explode, but not this time.

This time I was glad to be away from everyone else. Away from the noise. Away from the gossip. Away from the election. Away from my friends who hated me. Just ... *away*.

I was so okay with being alone that I didn't even care about keeping myself busy. I had stacks of assignments I could work on, but instead, I folded my arms on the table in front of me and buried my head in them.

'No sleeping in detention!' said a voice from the door.

The sudden sound scared me to death. I jerked to the side, completely sliding off my chair like a bumbling fool.

Melvin.

Shutting the door behind him, Melvin stepped into the room. He chuckled as he held his hand out to help me up.

'Such grace,' he said. 'I guess I can cross you off the list of people who I suspect are ninjas.'

I faked a laugh. 'Guess so,' I said, taking his hand and standing. 'What're you doing in here?'

'I thought you'd like to know that Brayden just dropped out of the election,' Melvin said. 'Obviously because of your video.'

'It wasn't *my* video,' I said, upset. Brayden was really looking forward to running for president. And now, because of me, his whole reputation had a muddy spot on it.

'No? Then whose video was it?'

I started to answer, but stopped. Fear of the Scavengers made me hold my tongue.

'That's what I thought.' Melvin sat on the chair next to me. 'Anyways, I wanted to ask you some questions about the ninja. Figured this was a good time to do it since you can't go anywhere.'

I gulped. 'Look, dude. I don't know what you're talkin' about.'

'But *you* were the one I was told to follow!'

'By some random text message?' I asked. 'How do you know it wasn't some kind of prank? How do you know that wasn't to keep you distracted from something else? Something bigger?'

Melvin's face grew serious. 'You've sparked my interest. What bigger thing?'

I hesitated for a moment, but decided that I just didn't care about keeping them a secret anymore. '*Scavengers.*'

Melvin choked out a laugh. 'Yeah, right! Like the Scavengers even exist!'

I looked at the reporter, surprised. '*Really?* Ninjas are hiding in the school halls, but a group of kids who call themselves the Scavengers is unbelievable?'

'Ghost stories,' Melvin said arrogantly. 'The Scavenger rumours only exist to keep kids from unloading their life story in a note to a friend.'

'What if I told you,' I said, 'that the Scavengers are real?'

'I would look you in the eye,' Melvin replied. 'And say poppycock!'

I laughed. 'You're following the wrong story. It's not ninjas you need to worry about. It's the Scavengers. They're real, and they know everything about everyone.'

Melvin shook his head, tapping on the desk. 'Alright, smart guy. Tell me about the "Scavengers",' he said, making air quotes with his fingers.

I glanced over my shoulder. I had to double check we were alone.

Melvin let out a huff. It was a short laugh, obviously he thought I was being dumb.

Finally, I said, 'You think I'm running in this race on purpose?'

'Yes,' Melvin said flatly.

'Well,' I said, 'I'm *not*. They entered me.'

'Why?' Melvin asked, rolling his eyes.

I curled my lip. 'Because they want revenge.'

'You mean the Scavengers are seeking vengeance by having you run for class president? That sounds a little…over the top.'

I nodded slowly, staring at the reporter with the most intense eyes I could muster.

'Do you know how *coconuts* that sounds?' Melvin asked, not even trying to hide a smile. He started speaking with a lower voice, impersonating what he thought a Scavenger sounded like. 'Oh, we hate Chase Cooper. Here's an idea! Let's have him run for president! That'll teach him a lesson! Oh, the sweet taste of revenge!'

'Whatever, dude.'

'Man, if that's how the Scavengers get their revenge,' Melvin said, 'sign me up! How can I make them angry too?'

I folded my arms and pushed against the back of my chair…yes, like a baby. 'It's because I exposed Sebastian for lying to the students and staff last week.'

Melvin lifted his head steadily. 'Sebastian was a Scavenger?'

'Yup.'

The reporter pushed his lips to the side of his face and lifted an eyebrow. With a thumbs up, he sarcastically said, 'Yeah, *okay*. That sounds like something that would happen.'

'You think it sounds crazy, but you're looking for *ninjas*! Tell me that's not crazy!'

'Ninjas are a totally different animal,' Melvin said. 'Plus there's already photographic evidence that they exist.'

'Just a kid in a Halloween costume,' I said. Hopefully the reporter couldn't see through my lies.

'Maybe, but that doesn't make them any less of a ninja. So tell me, Chase Cooper, why would I receive a text message telling me to follow you to learn the truth about the Buchanan ninjas?'

'What's your beef with ninjas anyway?' I asked.

Melvin paused, and then he whispered, 'My father was *kidnapped* by ninjas.'

I stared in disbelief. 'Whaaaat?'

'No, I'm joking,' Melvin laughed. 'But seriously, ninjas are dangerous, and the fact that they're hiding in our school is bad. Ninjas aren't good guys.'

'What if these ninjas are?'

'So you're saying there are ninjas in the school?'

I cleared my throat. 'No. I'm just saying that maybe you should consider it a possibility that you're wrong. Maybe not all ninjas are bad. Maybe the Scavengers are real. As a reporter, shouldn't you consider every angle?'

Melvin scribbled in his notepad. 'Fair enough.'

The door to the room swung open. Mr Lien stepped in and snatched some papers from his desk. He looked up, surprised to see Melvin. 'Excuse me? What're you doing in here?'

'Buchanan Press,' Melvin said boldly.

'I don't care if you're the president,' the teacher snipped. 'If you're not supposed to be in here, get out!'

Flipping his notepad shut, Melvin jumped from his seat. Before leaving the room, he said, 'We'll continue this later.'

Fantastic. *Another* thing to look forward to. That was sarcasm … in case you couldn't tell.

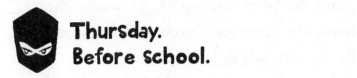

Thursday.
Before school.

The next morning, I crammed my book bag into my locker. Since I was going to be on the clean-up crew all day, I figured I didn't need anything with me.

I passed Brayden in the hallway but he didn't even acknowledge my existence. Dirty looks I can handle. Mean comments I can handle. Even getting punched in the face I can *kind* of handle. But acting like I didn't even exist was far worse than any of those other things.

When I stepped into the lobby, a bunch of kids cheered, '*Coopster for president!*', but I just wasn't into it. All I wanted was for Friday night to come along so I could lose myself in video games and comic books. The weekend was starting to sound really good.

Suddenly, a kid from Jake's wolf pack accidentally bumped into me. He was cutting across the lobby, looking like he was on the hunt. His name was Devon, and he was one of the meaner kids in Jake's posse.

Across the room, I saw Melvin drinking from a water fountain – one where the water barely makes it out of the tap so you practically have to make out with the water fountain if you want a drink. So gross.

I let out a heavy sigh. As much as Melvin was getting on my nerves, I still didn't want the kid to get hurt, especially since he was clueless about the danger he was flirting with.

Keeping my head down, I followed Devon as he weaved between students in the busy lobby.

Melvin slurped at the water like a thirsty dog. His ginormous camera slung over his shoulder, resting at his side.

As Devon got closer, I sped up, cutting around a few students so I could pass him without being seen. In his hand was a roll of duct tape, probably for taping Melvin to a wall. What a weird thing for bullies to do.

I was about three metres away when Melvin finally rose from the water fountain. Using his sleeve, he wiped the water from his mouth and began turning around.

I heard the ripping sound of duct tape as Devon raised his hands higher. There wasn't any time left. I had to act fast.

Jumping through an open spot in the crowd, I landed in front of the bully, blocking his path to Melvin. I grabbed the tape before Devon knew what was happening.

Spinning a circle in the hall, I rolled my fists around both of Devon's wrists. Since I was spinning, I rolled the tape around his hands once when they were in front of me, and then again when they were behind me, and finally one last time when they were in front of me again. It was almost like I was dancing.

I had used Devon's own trap against him.

'Hey!' Devon grunted.

We were still moving forward so all I had to do was nudge him once when we had passed the water fountain. He lumbered into the girls' bathroom door, pushing it open, and falling inside.

The screams and shouts from the girls' bathroom made me laugh, and also made sure Devon was gonna get busted.

A small crowd gathered around the bathroom door as I walked away from it. Melvin was clear down the hallway, completely clueless that I had saved him from trouble.

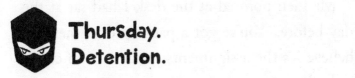

Thursday.
Detention.

Principal Davis had put me on clean-up duty for the day, which was exactly what it sounded like. I was going to be parading around the school grounds wearing a hi-vis vest and hat, picking up litter. Super fun, right?

I was slipping the vest on when Mr Lien came into the room. He was carrying a box with empty rubbish bags and a rubbish picker – one of those long handles with a set of pincers on the end that people use to pick up rubbish without bending over. I gotta be honest – I was excited to play with it.

Someone dashed past the door, dropping a large stack of papers in front of the room. It was probably the school paper. Melvin didn't have the goods on the ninjas yet so I wasn't worried about any articles he might've written.

Mr Lien pointed at the desk I had sat at the day before. 'You've got a package over there. I believe it's the assignments you'll miss in class today.'

I studied the package, which was about the size of a shoebox. No way a day's worth of homework could fill such a huge container.

'As soon as you're ready, you're free to walk the schoolyard and pick up rubbish,' Mr Lien said before he left.

'Gotcha,' I replied. Finally, I was alone with the mystery box.

I jabbed at it with my finger. Whatever was inside wasn't heavy because the box spun in a half circle.

I ripped the lid of the box off. I stared at the contents, confused.

Sitting on top of several folded sheets of paper was a note I had written to Faith a few months back. Some might call it a love note, but I'd call it a like note, got it?

I took my note out of the box, surprised to see it. When I looked closer, I saw that it was a photocopy.

Tipping the box over, I emptied the rest of the folded sheets of paper onto the desk. They were all black and white photocopies of love notes from random students in the school. I was standing above a gossip treasure chest.

The television in the hallway switched on, playing music through the school's speaker system. As I approached the door, I listened to the message that the whole school was hearing.

'Buchanan School...' the narrator said. It was the same voice that was in the video about Brayden. 'A place where friendships are tested in the waters of gossip and rumours. A place where secrets can tear relationships apart the same way babies tear into a bag of chips.'

My face – my goofy, smiling face – slowly appeared on the screen. I wasn't surprised.

What were the Scavengers going to say today? What friend were they going to try to take away from me this time?

The narrator continued. 'Which is why Chase Cooper has promised to *end* all secrets. If nobody has secrets, then we're one big happy family. That's what Chase is offering to the school!'

'Zoinks,' I whispered. 'Did I just say "zoinks"? Who am I even talking to?'

'That's why the Chase Cooper newsletter has been distributed to everyone!' the voice said enthusiastically. 'It highlights the juiciest secrets that your friends have to offer! Read up, kids! A friend who keeps secrets isn't a friend at all! So let's *all* be BFFs! You're welcome, Buchanan. You're welcome.'

I looked down at the stack of papers that were dropped off by the front door before class started. It wasn't the school paper I was staring at. It was the *Chase Cooper Newsletter of Secrets*, complete with a huge bold title and everything.

The video started to fade out, but not before my recorded voice played over the speakers again. *'My name is Chase Cooper, and I approve this message.'*

Holy. Stromboli.

I knew it was bad because just on the front page, I could see several secrets highlighted. The ones that stuck out were the ones about the people I knew.

Naomi has kissed a boy.
Brayden sleeps with a nightlight.
Jake has an unnatural fear of clowns.
Gavin barfs at the sight of barf.
Olivia Jones pretends to be a villain named
Jovial Noise.
Wyatt wet the bed until he was seven years old.

The list went on when I unfolded the newspaper. This was *bad*. *Super* bad. Like *end-of-the-world-because-the-sun-just-exploded* bad.

I could hear shrieks of terror echo down the hall as students poured from their classrooms. Homeroom wasn't over, but that didn't stop them.

Slinking back into detention, I shut the door quietly, locking it. I could hear the mob grow angrier through the thin walls of the room.

So that's the friend the Scavengers were going to take from me – *all of them*.

 **Thursday.
Lunch.**

I waited until first period started before I left
the detention room. Mr Lien didn't even try to
convince me to come out earlier. In fact, he
encouraged me to stay in there all day, but being
in that tiny room made me feel like a caged
animal. If there was anything I needed, it was
some fresh air. I made a deal with Mr Lien to
stay out of sight, at least until lunch.

Principal Davis made sure all the newsletters
were rounded up and stored them away in the
detention room until they could be properly
recycled.

But I had to get away from the smell of the newsprint. They were musty and reeked of burnt ink. Whatever the ink was that they used was weird. I'm sure the ink would be settled on the newsprint within a couple of hours, but it was still fresh enough that it got all over my fingers, which then got *everywhere*. My book bag, clothing and face had black streaks all over them. I looked like I cleaned chimneys for a living.

The only good thing about it was that nobody recognised me when I walked to the kitchen.

But even though they didn't see me, they still talked about me.

'Can't believe Chase would do such an awful thing.'

'Right? He better get expelled or I'm going to petition.'

'If we get enough signatures, I bet we could make it happen!'

Jeez. Crazy how fast fans can turn to haters.

Grabbing my yellow lunch tray, I stepped out

of the kitchen and into the cafeteria. I stood in the doorway for a second, waiting to see if anyone would know it was me. I was safe since my face had newspaper ink all over it. Not much of a disguise, but it seemed to be working.

At the far corner of the cafeteria, I found an empty table and sat, but I didn't feel hungry. It was fried chicken leg day anyway – not my favourite food.

'Eating in the cafeteria?' Naomi asked, appearing out of nowhere. She stood over me with her hands behind her back. 'Awfully brave of you.'

I winced. Apparently the printer ink on my face *wasn't* enough of a disguise. 'Is it obvious that it's me?'

Naomi smiled. 'Nah,' she said softly. 'Just to me. I could tell it was you if you were wearing a gorilla costume.' Studying me, her expression softened like she felt sorry for me. 'But man, you look *terrible*. How'd your clothes get all dirty?'

'Detention will do that to ya,' I said. 'I've *seen* things, Naomi. *Sickening* things.'

'Like what?'

'A dead mouse.'

'Ew, *barf-aroni*! Really?'

'Well, not the actual dead mouse itself,' I said. 'But I could smell it. Have you ever smelled a dead mouse? That's not somethin' you can easily come back from.'

'Well, ya look like you're about to play some football,' Naomi said.

'Yeah, because that sounds like me,' I said, looking at my fingers. 'No, I got newspaper ink all over my hands from that dumb newsletter.

The ink was all powdery and messy still. It's impossible to get off and gets *everywhere*.'

'Oh?' Naomi said, lifting an eyebrow. 'I wouldn't know. I didn't touch any of those papers.'

I let out a sigh. 'Man, I wish I didn't touch any either.'

'So it wasn't you that printed them?' Naomi asked jokingly.

'*Really?*' I replied.

Out of nowhere, a mound of wet mashed potatoes exploded on the table next to us. Other students at nearby tables turned in their seats to see what had made the *splut* sound.

Someone shouted from across the room. 'Hey, everybody! It's the Coopster! The Coopster's dumb enough to eat lunch in here!'

Chicken legs started travelling in my direction – probably the only food *designed* to be chucked across a vast open space. They were like fried grenades sailing across a battlefield of frustrated sixth graders. I was just thankful that nobody had good aim.

'Get out of here, loser!' a girl shouted. 'Because of you, everyone knows I had head lice in third grade! My boyfriend dumped me after he read that in your little gossip magazine!'

Everyone started screaming at the same time. I could only make out small bits here and there, but the general gist was how much they hated me.

Pushing my tray aside, I jumped up and ran.

I heard Naomi yell after me, but I didn't slow down. I ran all the way down the side of the cafeteria, dodging handfuls of food and ignoring the angry howls from the mob that had formed in the lunchroom.

Slamming my body into the door, I stumbled into the lobby, safe from the other students. But that wasn't far enough for me. Keeping my face down, I escaped into one of the nearby bathrooms.

My heart was pumping so hard that my eyes could *see* it. Every pump of blood made the lights in the bathroom dim just a little. I could count my pulse by watching the shadows on the wall.

Sliding my hand against the wall stopped me from falling over, but my knees were starting to feel weak. I kicked open one of the stall doors and locked it behind me.

My mouth started watering like crazy, and then I finally did what I had always been afraid of doing in school.

I barfed.

Good thing I was already in the stall, right?

It wasn't much, but I felt *wrecked*. Flushing the toilet, I climbed up and sat on the tank, wiping my mouth with toilet paper and catching my breath.

It was at that moment I heard the bathroom door swing open.

I swallowed hard, and waited patiently for whoever it was to do their business and leave. If I just sat silently, they wouldn't even know I was in there.

Except that whoever it was knocked on the stall door that I was in.

I froze. Even on a normal day, if someone knocked on a bathroom stall door that I was in, I would freak out. 'Uh, um…occupied,' I said, staring at the bright red tennis shoes that were standing at the foot of the stall door.

And then the most bizarre thing happened. The latch to the stall I was in slowly started moving to the left on its own. The door was unlocking itself.

Clunk.

All I could do was stare at the door as it slowly opened.

On the other side stood a boy, at least I think it was a boy, wearing a vulture mask. He was holding a small magnet. That must be how he managed to slide the lock open from the outside.

'Dude,' I said, upset that someone had just opened my *locked* stall door. '*What if I was in here droppin' the kids off at the pool?*'

The vulture mask tilted, the same way a dog's head does when they're confused. 'Kids? Pool?'

'Number two!' I snapped.

'Oh,' the boy said, shaking his head. 'I dunno. I'm only here to deliver a message.'

'They told you to deliver it while I was on the john?' I growled. 'That's insane.'

'It is what it is,' the boy replied.

'But what if it isn't what it is?' I asked. 'Or wasn't what it used to be, but became what it was supposed to be?'

The Scavenger held his open palm out to me, motioning for me to stop. 'Please,' he said, shaking his head. 'You're going to make my brain cry.'

'Who's your leader?' I asked, hoping the boy would be confused enough to answer without thinking.

The boy ignored my question, stuttering just a bit as he spoke. It sounded as if he were reciting something he memorised. 'If... if you *tell* on us, we'll move in on your friends. Zoe, Faith, Brayden, Naomi and Gavin.'

My blood boiled.

'They will all fall victim to the wrath of the Scavengers,' he said. 'We'll allow you to lose with *some* shred of your dignity left. We'll end this game with you, leaving your friends alone, *if* you accept defeat.'

I leaned back against the cold wall, staring into the eyes of the boy in the mask.

'Become the nobody that you should've been when you showed up on the first day of school.'

My eyes drifted to the floor as I listened.

'We're giving you a second chance to become *nothing*,' the boy said. 'To be the student who just disappears in a sea of other students.'

I clenched my jaw as the masked kid shut the stall door. He stomped across the bathroom to the door, opening it and walking out. I heard the noise from students in the hall, waiting for lunch to end. Then it was silent again.

My throat dried up as I stared at nothing. The quiet and stillness of the empty restroom felt like it was going to crush my head so I flushed the toilet again just to hear *something*.

The Scavengers had done what no other student had done to me – destroyed my reputation. But they did it in a way that I couldn't even fight back. I felt completely helpless.

But I didn't want it to end like that.

Squeezing my eyes shut as tight as I could, I felt a surge of energy travel down my back. *Why* couldn't I fight back? *Why* couldn't I do something about it?

Of course if I hid away in the bathroom then *nothing* would change! I was in charge of my own destiny, and I wasn't about to let a bunch of kids wearing ugly bird masks get the best of me!

I booted the stall door open and ran to the entrance of the bathroom. If I hurried, I could probably see the boy who delivered the message still walking away. He would've removed the vulture mask, but I'd still be able to recognise his bright red shoes.

When I pushed open the bathroom door, I felt like I was ready to take on the world, but it wasn't the world waiting on the other side. It was Jake and Wyatt.

Jake shoved me back onto the wall. 'You didn't think I'd forgot about the payback I owed you, didya? I was just waiting for the right time!'

Wyatt stood like a statue behind Jake. 'You're gonna pay so bad for that paper you put out this morning! The fact that I wet my bed until I was seven is nobody's business but my own!'

'Tell him, babe!' muttered Olivia. As a crowd of students started gathering around us, I

couldn't see her anymore, but I heard her start chanting again. 'Wy-att! Wy-att! Wy-att!'

I tried to respond, but it only came out as a jumble of vowels. My thoughts were drowning out any quirky comeback I tried to think of.

Instead of letting myself get pummelled, I rolled to my feet, dashing for the cafeteria door. I wasn't sure how many times I'd been involved in a chase within the walls of Buchanan School, but I knew it was going to be at least once more.

As I reached for the handle of the cafeteria door, I made an escape plan in my head. I was going to pull a sharp right turn after jumping through the entrance. After that, I'd sprint towards the stage. A sharp left turn would put me on a clear path to the exit at the back of the cafeteria. All I had to do was make it to the exit so I could get outside. Then it would be smooth sailing from there...

But it's funny how a small bump can toss an entire escape plan into the dumpster.

Just before I touched the handle to the

cafeteria door, someone pushed me. Since I was already running at full speed, I couldn't stop myself. My face smashed into the wooden door as my body crashed through the doorway.

I managed to keep myself on my feet, but not without looking like a puppet that was being forced to dance for a roomful of students.

Finally, because the universe hates me, I slammed into one of the lunch tables, which sent me flying over the top of it like a stuntman earning his salary.

On my back, I stared at the ceiling of the school, listening to the roar of laughter erupting from my peers.

The faces of kids became blurs as I blinked, trying to keep a straight face through the sharp pain of getting tossed around like a ragdoll.

The worst part about it? I knew it was all *my* fault – all of it. If I had just minded my own business at the beginning of the year, I wouldn't be the laughing stock of the whole lunchroom. I wouldn't be on my back contemplating a transfer to another school. I wouldn't be running my tongue over all my teeth, making sure none of them were missing.

Basically, I wouldn't have any troubles.

As I forced myself off the ground, I could hear every insult that everyone was throwing at me. I'm sure there were teachers who were trying to help me, but the crowd of spectators was so thick that it didn't make it easy.

Zoe pushed through the mob, and stopped just at the edge of it. 'Chase…?'

I couldn't stand it anymore. The

embarrassment was so heavy and maddening that I ran to the stage at the front of the room. I rolled across the wood and escaped under the red velvet curtain.

But I could still hear everyone's laughter and taunts so I continued until I was as far backstage as I could go.

There in the dark, I leaned against one of the wooden storage boxes. It sucks saying this, but I was trying my hardest to hold in my tears. With my luck, if I started crying, the curtains would split open and a spotlight would shine on me.

Suddenly footsteps pounded on the stage, but they weren't close. I pushed my back against the box, making myself as small as possible so I wouldn't be seen.

Whoever was running was panting heavily. I peeked over the box to see what was going on.

Across the stage, Melvin was running at full speed, his camera swinging wildly on his shoulder. Behind him were two red ninjas.

I slapped the wooden floor of the stage, frustrated. My brain started arguing with me as I tried to shut out the sound of Melvin's footsteps.

Go help him!

'Why?' I asked aloud.

Y'know, ninja honour and stuff.

'I mean, I *know* why! But why should I bother? Everyone at this school hates me!'

So what? This isn't about who hates you and who doesn't! This is about doing the right thing, even when you don't feel like it!

'But what's the right thing?' I asked, like I was actually talking to someone. 'What if sitting here was the right thing? What if doing nothing to help him is the right thing? Hmm?'

If you don't help Melvin, I'm going to make you think of your parents kissing!

'Gross, dude!'

I swear I'll do it!

'Whatever! You can't make me do that!'

Oh really? Watch this – DON'T think of your parents kissing!

My pupils dilated as the world went black. '*Noooo!*'

Now go!

I paused, pulling my ninja mask over my face. 'What if he doesn't even need help?'

My brain didn't answer.

I furrowed my brow, looking up like I was going to actually see my own brain. I shook my head, realising how insane I must've looked.

I grunted, picking myself up off the floor. Melvin might've been an annoying insect, but he didn't deserve to get beat up for doing his job – nobody did … unless their job was pro-wrestling, but last I checked, Melvin *wasn't* a pro-wrestler.

Unless he was a secret pro-wrestler that was parading around as a— Nope, never mind.

I glanced down the short corridor that the red ninjas had chased Melvin down. It was a hallway full of exits, but I could still hear their footsteps. It meant Wyatt and Jake were back there, and probably gaining on the reporter.

I took off running towards the sound of the steps. 'It's go time.'

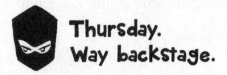

Thursday.
Way backstage.

'Melvin, Melvin, Melvin,' sighed one of the red ninjas. 'We warned you. You had the chance to just… forget about it, but you chose not to.'

'The students of the school need to know the truth!' Melvin shouted, hanging upside down. 'I *knew* there were ninjas in this school! I totally called it!'

Melvin was slung over one of the overhead catwalks by thick rope around his ankle. The place where the red ninjas had tied the knot was only a metre away from me.

I was sticking to the shadows on the catwalk,

167

looking down on the red ninjas and the reporter. I didn't have a plan, but I knew I needed one quick or Melvin was going to pass out.

One of the red ninjas pushed Melvin, making him swing back and forth slowly.

'Ever heard of a piñata?' the red ninja snarled. 'I wonder … will you spill some candy if we pop you open?'

The other ninja chuckled, keeping his arms folded. It looked as bizarre and evil as it sounded.

'You know,' the first ninja said, kneeling closer to Melvin's face, 'our clan could use a new punching bag.'

'You think you can get away with this?' Melvin asked, his voice shaking.

The two ninjas looked at each other. After a few nods back and forth, the shorter ninja looked at Melvin. 'Yeah,' he said. 'Yeah, we do.'

I knew who they were from their voices, especially since I had just dealt with them in the lobby. It was Wyatt, the leader of the red ninjas, and Jake, the leader of the wolf pack.

Quickly and quietly, I untied the knot on the thick rope next to me. I had to wrap it around my arm a few times. With my feet, I propped myself against the catwalk so I could carry Melvin's weight without him dropping to the floor.

Melvin's camera was on the ground, just out of his reach. Wyatt danced over to it.

'Don't think you'll be needing *this* anymore!' he sang as he booted it like he was trying to score a goal.

The old camera shot across the floor and smashed into pieces against a brick wall. A flash of light and a puff of smoke burst from the camera.

'No!' Melvin shouted. 'That thing was an antique!'

'Get with the times!' Jake hissed. 'Use a camera phone like everyone else in the world!'

'I *have* a camera phone,' Melvin said. 'But I prefer old school!'

Wyatt chuckled. 'The 1800s called, Mel! They want their camera back!'

Melvin's face was growing red, maybe from being angry, but probably from hanging upside down too long. 'Gross. My dad called – he wants his lame joke back.'

I couldn't see Wyatt's face, but I knew Melvin's comment had instantly angered him from the way his posture changed. He planted one foot behind him. 'Insulting me is the last mistake you'll ever make!'

That was it – the sign that things had escalated from a mean prank to red alert.

Holding the rope tight in both of my hands, I did one of the most dangerously irresponsible things in my life. I jumped over the side of the catwalk.

I instantly regretted it, crying out in fear.

'Gaaaah! Look out!'

If this were a movie, I would've landed on my feet, using Melvin's weight to counter my own to allow for a smooth descent. But since this was real life, I dropped like a sack of potatoes.

Melvin's weight on the other end of the rope was at least enough that I didn't break any bones. That, plus landing on top of him probably helped too. It was clumsy, awkward and painful.

But it was awesome.

Wyatt and Jake stepped back, surprised by my sudden ninja-like entrance.

Melvin whimpered under me. It's possible that I might've done more damage to him than Jake and Wyatt were going to do.

'Sorry, man,' I said. 'Please don't be dead.'

The reporter pushed me. 'Get off me!'

Rolling to my feet, I stuck out my chest and stared at the two red ninjas.

The confusion left Wyatt's eyes – it was almost like I could see the light bulb switch on in his head. 'Enjoy your trip back in the cafeteria?'

I couldn't think of a good comeback, so instead, I said, 'Not really.'

Jake stepped forward, his muffled voice speaking through his red ninja mask. 'Why are you protecting Melvin? Don't you understand that this involves both our clans? If he exposes one, he exposes *both*! Don't you want to stop him?'

'I'm not a fan of Melvin's intentions,' I said. 'But this isn't the way to stop him.'

Wyatt chuckled. 'You think asking nicely will work?' He leaned over, resting his hands on his knees and spoke to Melvin in a baby voice. 'Pwetty pwease, with sugah on top?'

Melvin's stare grew intense, but he didn't say anything.

Suddenly, Jake pushed me hard. I stumbled, trying to avoid Melvin, but I tripped over his body and fell onto the wooden floor.

Melvin jumped up, grabbing my arm and helping me to my feet. 'Hit them back! Give them what they deserve!'

I didn't have time to tell Melvin my belief that punches should never be thrown, so instead, I said nothing. I walked backwards, keeping him behind me.

Wyatt jumped through the air, coming at me with his legs scissor-kicking like a weird-looking flamingo. He even made the same sound a flamingo would make, but I'm not a hundred per cent sure about that – I'm not an expert on flamingos.

I pushed Melvin back, trying to keep him safe from the attack. The reporter grabbed my hoodie, clinging to me like a child. Because of that, I hobbled over him, tripping again.

I managed to stay on my feet, but just as I had caught my balance, Jake slammed into Melvin and me.

We stumbled into the door at the side of the room. It was old and crusty, so instead of breaking our fall, we broke it. Wood splintered everywhere as Melvin and I crashed into the next room.

Someone screamed, frightened by our sudden appearance. I'm not surprised – kids crashing through doors isn't something you see every day.

'Where are we?' I asked, rubbing my head.

'The voting room,' Melvin said as he lay on his back.

At the far corner of the room, Daisy was holding a cardboard box upside down, dumping a ton of pink slips into a giant red machine.

'Daisy?' I asked through my ninja mask.

Before she could answer, Jake and Wyatt

stepped into the room still decked out in their red ninja gear.

Daisy's eyes bulged open like a cartoon, and she let out the loudest scream I'd ever heard in my life.

Melvin scooted across the floor trying to get away from the two red ninjas. He had his phone out and was snapping pictures. Bright flashes flooded my vision as I tried to make sense of what was happening.

'Leave him alone!' I shouted, pushing myself off the floor.

Jake turned and threw a roundhouse kick in my direction. If I were closer, it probably would've done some damage, but since I was just out of reach, his foot swung wildly, unable to stop. It was like when a kid swings a baseball bat too hard, but misses the ball. Jake lost his balance and tumbled to the floor.

'*Nothin' but net!*' I said like an announcer.

All of the commotion in the room halted. Everyone looked at me in confusion.

Even Daisy, who was crouched down picking up her pink slips, stopped.

'I think "nothin' but net" would mean that the ninja totally kicked you,' Melvin said.

Wyatt nodded. '"Nothin' but net" is a good thing.'

'Oh,' I said, scratching the back of my head. 'Um, so...'

'I think you meant to say "air ball",' Melvin said.

I snapped my fingers at the reporter. 'That's it! That's what I meant! *Aiiiiir ball!*'

Jake picked himself up off the ground. 'Can we continue this then?'

I looked at Melvin and shrugged. Melvin looked at Wyatt and they both nodded.

It was such a strange pause in all the action that I honestly believe the whole fight would've ended there if it weren't for Daisy sparking the flame back into a fire.

Daisy tossed her cardboard box to the ground and ran for the exit. Several slips of pink paper fell from her box. Wyatt moved towards Daisy.

'No!' Daisy screamed, reaching for the handle.

I was too far away to do anything.

Suddenly, the door swung open before Daisy had even touched it. Someone on the outside must've opened it. As soon as she ran out, the door slammed shut again.

Wyatt slid to a stop, confused. He stared at the door like it was going to open again, but it stayed closed.

Melvin was still cowering in the corner snapping photos on his phone.

Jake was beginning to panic too.

I was on the floor, frozen in confusion, which is why I didn't notice Jake moving towards Melvin until the very last second.

'Help!' Melvin shouted, snapping pictures of Jake.

I dashed across the room. I wasn't sure what my plan was, but I didn't have time to think about it.

With my arms in front of me, I jumped at Jake, but he was ready for me and dodged. After I hit the ground, he ignored me, continuing his pursuit of Melvin.

'Gimme that phone!' Jake shouted as he raised his fists.

I grabbed Jake's ankle and yanked him off his balance. He whipped his hands out behind him to keep himself from falling. He glared at me through his mask. 'I am *so* sick of you being *everywhere*!'

He reached for Melvin's phone, but I jumped in the way. Instead of grabbing the phone, Jake grabbed the top of my mask and clenched his fist.

'You want a story?' Jake sneered at Melvin. 'How's *this*?'

Jake ripped my ninja mask off my face. The blast of cold air from the room hit my face as Melvin gasped.

I pushed Jake off me, but he didn't care. He was laughing as he stumbled backward, gripping my black ninja mask in his hand.

Melvin's jaw was dropped. He was shocked, but not shocked enough to stop taking pics.

Wyatt clenched his fists, glaring at Jake. The really weird thing about Wyatt was that

while he was an evil dude, there were still rules he followed. A couple of weeks ago, I found out that one of his rules is never revealing the identity of another ninja, even if that ninja was me.

It's the ninja code, which is like the bro code, but with ninjas ... except the bro code means you don't date your best friend's ex-girlfriend sooo ... the ninja code is nothing like that.

Jake had just crossed the line.

A cloud of white dust exploded at the entrance. I heard the door swing open, along with the sound of several people shuffling around. The door clicked shut again.

As the dust cleared, black silhouettes came into view. There must have been at least ten shadows standing near the entrance with their arms folded.

After another second, it was clear that the room was filled with new ninjas – *my* ninjas. That must've been why Wyatt was shocked earlier – he caught a glimpse of them when they opened the door for Daisy.

'Leave,' said one of my ninjas. 'You don't want none of this.'

Jake lifted the bottom part of his mask and spat on the ground. He dropped my ninja mask. 'Next time use less chalk. It's bad for the lungs.'

Wyatt wasn't about to try his odds against ten members of my clan. He held his fingers up to Jake, signalling him to keep his mouth shut. Without a word, Wyatt stepped back through the door we had shattered.

Jake followed, shooting Melvin one last look.

I approached the members of my ninja clan. 'How'd you guys know we were in here?'

One of the ninjas hesitated. 'Master…'

I could tell he was hiding something. 'What is it?' I asked.

'This will be the last time we help you,' the ninja said, not sadly, but softly.

I looked at him, confused.

Melvin finally got the moment he had been waiting for. He grabbed several of the pink slips Daisy had dropped and darted for the exit, disappearing into the hall.

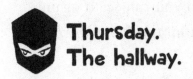 **Thursday.
The hallway.**

'Wait!' I shouted, reaching my hand out like
I was going to use the Force to stop Melvin.
I squeezed my hand shut, embarrassed. 'Dang
it!'

I pushed through my ninja clan and ran into
the lobby.

'Stay outta sight!' I said over my shoulder as
I chased after Melvin. 'Melvin, stop! Wait!'

Any response Melvin might've made was
masked by his high-pitched wheezing.

'Let me explain!' I shouted as I sprinted after
the reporter. At the end of the hallway, I cut

the corner without slowing down so I could keep up. 'Melvin, stop! I just want to talk to—'

BAM!

My skull met another kid's skull, but not in a 'It's nice to meet you!' sort of way. It was more of a 'Oh my god, did you see that? Let me rewind the video so you can see it again! Watch, watch, watch, annnnnnd...*Ohhhhh!*' kind of way.

The flash of pain was blinding as I crumpled to the floor. I heard a sharp cry of pain as someone hit the lockers. When the stars cleared from my vision, I saw Naomi leaning against the wall, holding her head.

'Thanks for that,' Naomi said, keeping her eyes shut. 'I don't understand why you still insist on running around corners at warp speed. You'd think that you would've learned a lesson after the first time you crashed into someone.'

'I was running after Melvin,' I said, pinching my nose, hoping that blood wouldn't start pouring out of it. 'Did you see him run back here?'

Naomi rubbed her forehead. 'Maybe? I'm having a hard time remembering anything before you head-checked me.'

I laughed, but realised she might not have been joking. 'Serious?'

'No,' Naomi said. 'I'm not serious.'

I crawled across the cold floor towards my friend's book bag that was crumpled on the linoleum next to us. 'Sorry about that,' I said.

Massaging the spot between her eyes, Naomi spoke. 'It's fine,' she said. 'Too bad Melvin got away.'

I started scooping up Naomi's notebooks and gel pens. 'Yeah,' I said. 'And he totally saw my face. I have to find him. If I don't, he might publish something that'll ruin my life…not like it's not already—' I stopped when I pulled Naomi's book bag open to put her stuff away.

My face grew hot as I stared into her bag, slack-jawed. Resting at the bottom of the canvas sack was a vulture mask. It was the same kind that the Scavengers wore.

Naomi opened her eyes. 'What's—' She stopped when she saw my face. Then she calmly said, 'Are you gaping at the vulture mask? It's one of the masks you got in that package.'

I felt a wave of relief wash over me, but the feeling quickly faded.

'I broke those in half…' I said softly. 'And then I tossed them into the rubbish.'

Naomi flipped over and crawled closer to me. Grabbing my wrist, she pulled my arm away from her bag.

'I know,' she said without missing a beat. 'I got one out of the bin. I took it home and fixed it.'

'But why?' I asked, puzzled.

'In case you needed it again,' Naomi said, softly smiling, gazing into my eyes like a lost kitten. Naomi had a tear forming in her eye.

It was almost like she *wanted* me to see she was crying.

'I'm sorry about running into you,' I said.

Naomi nodded, wiping the tear from her face.

A black streak appeared on her cheek where her thumb had rubbed.

'You got some…' I started saying, lifting my thumb to Naomi's face. I tried to clean the black spot off, but I only made it worse. I still had ink on my hands from the newsletters. Funny enough, the black streak I left on Naomi's cheek matched the streak she had left with her own thumb. In fact, they even spread over her skin exactly the same way…

Wait, what?

I stared into Naomi's eyes with my hand still on her cheek. Then I glanced at the spot on my wrist where she had pulled me away from her bag – a black powdery ink was smeared there too.

'Dude,' she said, pulling away. 'You can let go of me now, ya creeper.'

My words dried up in my throat as I stared at Naomi's hands. She had a black residue on her fingertips and under her nails. My heart started racing.

'Back in the cafeteria,' I said. 'You told me you didn't touch any of the newsletters.'

Naomi paused. 'I didn't.'

'The funny thing about newspaper ink,' I said, 'is that it's impossible to get off... and it gets *everywhere*.'

Naomi looked at her hands, and then changed the story. 'Oh, I mean, I might've picked up a copy after I talked to you in the cafeteria.'

'All the copies have been hidden away though. Principal Davis made sure of that.'

'Not all of them,' Naomi said defensively.

My brain was stuck. 'Naomi... you're making yourself sound *more* guilty.'

Her expression completely shifted, and she sat up straight, staring daggers at me. She zipped up her book bag and stood up, slinging the bag over her right shoulder.

I waited for Naomi to explain herself, but she didn't.

Instead, she turned around and started walking down the hall.

'Naomi!' I said, standing up.

She didn't answer.

'Naomi, stop!' I said, following her. 'Please! Why's that mask in your bag?'

Again, she didn't answer. She didn't even look over her shoulder at me. It was like I wasn't even there.

I jogged to catch up. Staying a couple of metres behind her, I pleaded with her. I didn't want my suspicion to be correct.

I didn't want my friend to be a Scavenger!

I grabbed her arm. 'Please talk to me!'

Naomi spun around, raising her elbow so that it was above my hand. Then she dropped her elbow straight down, pulling free from my grip. She turned and continued her robotic walk down the hall.

Standing still in the middle of the corridor, I watched as my friend, one of my *best* friends, ignored me.

At the end of the hall, she turned to her right and opened one of the doors. She glanced at me before stepping through. But instead of shutting the door behind her, she left it wide open like she wanted me to follow her.

I could barely feel my legs as I hurried to the open door. I wasn't sure what to expect in the dark room. All I knew was that Naomi was in there.

I didn't have to think about it as I stepped into the unknown.

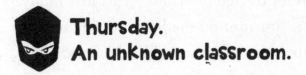

Thursday.
An unknown classroom.

'Naomi?' I whispered, walking further into the dark classroom. There weren't any windows to the outside to let light in, and the light switch on the wall didn't work. I flipped it a couple of times to make sure.

From the light in the hallway I could see props leaning against the walls. It looked like I was in one of the rooms for theatre class. There were cardboard cut-outs of castle walls and wooden gates.

When I was a good distance into the room, the door shut behind me, and I was left in darkness.

'Naomi? C'mon, please talk to me. What's going on?'

Something cranked from across the room, and then a spotlight blinded my vision as it pointed right at me. I raised my hand to shield myself from the light. 'Naomi? This isn't funny anymore. Just turn on the lights so we can talk.'

'So talk,' Naomi's voice said behind me.

I turned to look at her. She was seated on a golden throne that had decorations all over the arms and back. Behind her stood several students and behind them was a brick wall with a sign that read 'Brackenbury Lane' with an arrow pointing to the left.

I let out a short laugh when I realised it was the same brick wall we saw where room 001 was supposed to be in the Dungeon. The wall was fake. *That's* why Naomi didn't want me to knock on the bricks! Because I would've realised it wasn't real!

In Naomi's hand was the mask that was in her book bag, but she didn't put it on. Instead, she tossed it to the side. I focused on the

shadowed students behind her, and although I couldn't see their faces, I knew they weren't wearing their masks either.

I had never felt more betrayed in my life. 'What is this? Please tell me this is a joke.'

'You weren't supposed to find out yet,' Naomi said.

'Don't say that,' I said, feeling my heart break. 'This whole thing is just a big dumb prank, isn't it? A big dumb prank that's lasted for over two weeks, right?'

Naomi didn't say anything.

'Come on!' I said. 'This isn't real! You're not a Scavenger! You're my friend! You're one of my best ninjas! You're *afraid* of the Scavengers! You were so paranoid when I got their notes! You kept telling me to stay away from them! They even aired *your* secrets!'

'All necessary for you to believe I was on your team,' Naomi said. 'Besides, those are secrets I don't care if anyone knows. So I had a crush on you – big whoop.'

I shook my head at her, feeling a knot in my throat that wouldn't go down. 'No, this isn't real. This isn't you!'

'Like I said,' Naomi said, 'you weren't supposed to find out…*yet*.'

'I don't believe you,' I said, pointing at the kids behind Naomi. 'None of you guys are wearing those vulture masks. If you were Scavengers, you'd be working hard to hide your identity!'

Naomi laughed, as did the rest of the Scavengers behind her.

'The masks were a joke,' she said. 'It was all part of the act to scare you. Nobody here cares about hiding their identity. We're all pretty good at keeping secrets,' she said with a wink. 'We just found those masks in one of the drama club boxes and thought it'd be funny to wear them.'

'No!' I shouted, refusing to believe her. 'Stop this right now! This isn't funny! If you're working with the Scavengers, you've been trashing my life this whole week! You've *helped* them do this to me! And that's not something I can believe!' I grew angrier. 'Naomi, we're *friends*!'

'Chase,' Naomi said. 'I'm not *helping* them... I'm the *leader* of the Scavengers. *I'm* the one giving the orders!'

I felt the weight of everything press on my shoulders. It was too heavy for me to carry anymore, and I dropped to my knees. 'Since when?' I asked.

'Since the first day of school,' Naomi answered honestly.

'No,' I said. 'You've been a member of my ninja clan the whole time.'

'Doesn't it make sense that the Scavengers would have a spy in your ninja clan?' Naomi said. 'I wouldn't be the leader of the Scavengers if I didn't have my hand in everyone's cookie jar. But remember at the start of the year it was still Wyatt's clan.'

'Did Wyatt know?'

Naomi laughed. 'That kid is the most clueless twerp in the school. Of course he didn't know!'

My brain was melting. I've known Naomi since the second week of school. How was it possible that I didn't see this? How could I have missed something so huge? There's no way she was *that* good, was there?

'But I don't understand,' I said. 'You helped me bust Sebastian last week...'

Naomi shook her head. 'No, you did that on your own. You figured out his entire plan by yourself. I did nothing to help you.'

'But you didn't do anything to *stop* me,' I said.

'I told you to stay out of it!' Naomi replied. 'If I said anything more than that, I risked being discovered.'

I couldn't help myself, stepping forward and pointing an accusing finger at the girl I *used* to be friends with. '*Was this your plan the entire time?*'

The students around Naomi flinched, ready to stop me if I moved any closer.

Naomi held her hand up calmly, telling them to relax. 'Don't worry, he's harmless. He wouldn't hurt a fly.' She looked at me. 'To be honest, the last two weeks have been quite a ride for me too. For the first time since the beginning of the year, I didn't know what to expect, but I knew things were changing and it was exciting. After you got Sebastian fired, we needed to replace him with another Scavenger.'

'That's why you wanted to recruit me,' I said. 'And you were by my side the whole time *pretending* to be my friend.'

'We seriously wanted you to join us, but when you rejected our offer to make you president,' Naomi said, 'we had to go with another student.'

I thought for a moment. 'Daisy…'

'There's no need to hide the truth from you anymore,' Naomi said. 'Daisy is your replacement. When we offered her a place with us, she jumped at the chance, which is what I was hoping *you* would've done. And now she's winning the election and another Scavenger will become the president.'

'I guess it's true what they say,' I said.

The Scavengers glanced at each other, shrugging their shoulders.

Finally, Naomi spoke. 'Are you going to finish that thought?'

'Oh, right,' I said. 'Keep your friends close, and your enemies closer. You did a pretty good job of keeping me closer.'

'Chase,' Naomi said, sitting forward with a smile on her face. '*I'm* not your enemy. I want you to join the Scavengers! It's not too late. You're an *amazing* ninja, but you'd make a better Scavenger.'

I stared at the girl on the throne. The girl who I thought I could trust. The girl who used to be one of my closest friends.

'You've gone too far,' I whispered.

Naomi slammed her fist onto the arm of her throne. 'You left me no choice! I had to take everything from you!'

'*But why?*' I shouted.

'So you'd be left with no other option than to join us,' Naomi said. She lifted her hand to the Scavengers around her again. 'Step out of the shadows, guys.'

Naomi's followers did as she ordered, shuffling forward at the same time.

I couldn't believe what I was seeing. The Scavengers … were all members of my ninja clan.

'It's hard being a good leader,' Naomi said. 'Especially when you're never around.'

I looked at one of the boys in front. He was the one I was speaking to back in the voting room. 'But you just helped me get away from Jake and Wyatt.'

The boy lowered his head and spoke with the same tone that he used before, not sad, but soft. 'We're not against you, but we're not with you anymore. You've been absent from our training for too long.'

'Uh, duh!' I said, annoyed. 'Because I've had loads of trouble I was trying to get rid of! I'm juggling disasters every week!'

'We saved you from Jake and Wyatt,' the boy said, 'but that was the last time. We owed you at least that much.'

I started to respond, but Naomi cut me off.

'You haven't been to training for over two weeks!' Naomi said. 'And before that, you'd show up maybe once a week! These kids – these *ninjas* – wanted you to lead them, but you were never there.'

I wanted to argue, but I couldn't. She was right. I'd been so busy trying to save the school that I hardly showed up to ninja training. And between the situation with Sebastian and the Scavengers, I knew I had completely dropped the ball.

All I could do was apologise. 'I'm sorry.'

'Nobody's mad at you,' Naomi said softly. 'But I could see your ninjas needed direction, so I'm giving it to them.'

The whole thing was still blowing my mind. Not only had Naomi served me a piping hot dish of *betrayal*, but it also came with a cold glass of *take-my-ninja-clan-right-out-from-under-my-nose*. But she was acting like I was supposed to see this as a good thing!

It was like the way some people break up and pretend they're excited at being good friends afterwards. Yeah, right! Those two never speak to each other again.

'Join us,' Naomi said. 'You can end this.'

'You know I can't do that,' I replied, staring at the floor.

'Then stay out of our way,' Naomi said, 'or we'll tell the school that you're a ninja. And don't even *think* about telling anyone about us or we'll put them through everything you've been through.'

I sighed, realising that was the exact moment

that Naomi and I weren't going to be friends anymore. I said nothing else as I walked back to the exit.

'Once you walk out that door,' Naomi said from behind me, 'the invitation expires.'

Without another thought, I stepped through the door and into the hallway. I heard it latch shut behind me, and I was alone again.

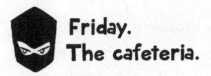 **Friday.
The cafeteria.**

My dad had to drop me off early the next
morning because the last part of my detention
was to help clean the cafeteria after breakfast.

I dragged my feet across the floor, sliding a
mop back and forth in front of me. I barely
slept a wink. I just couldn't get my mind off
Naomi and the Scavengers, plus all the other
million things that had blown up in my face.

I let my mind wander, thinking about what
exactly had happened this week.

First, the Scavengers offered me a place in
their creepy club. Rejecting them was the clap
that started the avalanche.

They put my name into the pot for presidency, which is what angered Zoe at first, but claiming her pizza party for my own was what turned her anger into hatred. Since Gavin was her boyfriend, he wasn't too happy with me either.

Brayden hated me because of the video that the whole school saw. He was so embarrassed of it that he dropped out of the race. My face twitched at the thought of Brayden *quitting* something because of how ashamed he was. I felt so bad about it.

And then came the *Chase Cooper Newsletter of Secrets*. That was the icing on the cake. That was how the Scavengers made everyone hate me.

But what hurt the most was that one of my best friends turned out to be someone they weren't. Naomi was someone I could trust, someone I could tell my secrets, someone I could count on to watch my back … and now that was gone.

The Naomi I knew was dead to me. No, that's not right – the Naomi I knew never existed. I thought about all those times she was by my side when Wyatt was being a butt, or when I needed to check out a hunch. All those times, she was just following me, *spying* on me.

Betrayed by someone I trusted ... bleh.

My thoughts went back to the ninja story I was daydreaming about earlier in the week – the one where I was on Scrag Seven rescuing Gwen from imprisonment.

'Chase?' Zoe's voice said.

Glancing over my shoulder, I saw my cousin standing with Gavin, Brayden and Faith.

'Hi,' I said, plopping my mop back into its bucket.

Zoe paused, looking at everyone else. Finally, she spoke.

'There's no way to do this without it being weird, but we all want to talk to you.'

'Before you do,' I said, 'I just want to apologise. Guys, I'm *so, so* sorry about this whole week.'

'That's what we wanted to talk to you about,' Zoe said, speaking for everyone. 'It's obvious that there's something going on with you, and even though you've been a total dork all week, well … we want you to know that we're still going to be there for you.'

'But why?' I asked, looking at the floor. 'Why bother with me? I'm a lost cause. Everyone hates me.'

Zoe leaned down so she could look me in the eye. 'Because that's what friends do. Friends make mistakes, and friends forgive. I'm not going to go into an "after-school special" style speech so don't make it weird. Just accept it and let's move forward.'

I looked at Gavin, Brayden and Faith. They nodded at me. Did I cry? No. Did I feel tears forming in my eyes? Maybe.

'Friendship means understanding when mistakes are made,' Zoe said. 'You've made some monster mistakes this week, but we all feel the same way about it: this week wasn't the same without you around to joke with. So could you stop making those mistakes and be cool again?'

And like that, some of the weight lifted off my shoulders. I didn't feel as alone or helpless as I did earlier. My face practically split in half with how big my smile was.

I remembered Naomi's threat about ruining my friends' lives like she ruined mine. And then, almost like she had planned it, I saw her peering through the tinted glass windows at the side of the cafeteria. She must've known what we were talking about because she put her finger to her lips and shook her head. Creepy much?

'All I can say is that everything that's happened this week,' I said to my friends, 'wasn't me.'

Brayden stepped forward. He had a smile on his face that I was glad to see. 'I *knew* it! I knew you weren't evil enough to make a video like that.'

I burst out laughing, almost explosively. For the first time all week, I felt normal again. 'That's all I can say though,' I said. 'At least for now.'

Zoe folded her arms. 'This is dumb. Just tell

us what's going on already. You've been a real jerk this whole time, and I think you owe us an explanation!'

I nodded. 'You're right, but I just … I can't. Please, believe me when I say I *want* to tell you.'

My cousin shook her head, disappointed. 'Fine. Be that way. Whatever it is can wait. Right now we have a cafeteria to clean.'

Everyone grabbed some cleaning supplies and started wiping down tables and sweeping the floors.

When Faith and I were far from the group, she smiled at me. 'Rough week, huh?'

I nodded. 'You don't know the half of it.'

'Maybe I know something about it,' she said. 'Secrets are hard to keep in this school.'

'You're tellin' me,' I said. 'How much do you know?'

'Enough to know you're not the one pulling the strings on your campaign,' Faith said. 'It's like you're a puppet, getting pulled left and right without any power to stop it.'

I glanced back at the tinted windows to make sure Naomi wasn't still watching. I couldn't see her anywhere. 'But...how do you know?'

'It wasn't hard to figure out.'

'Unless you were following me around the school, you couldn't possibly know about all I've been through,' I said.

Faith winked as she walked away. 'Let's just say you're not the only one with a secret identity as a ninja.'

'No, I'm sure I'm—' I stopped. 'Wait, what?' Faith didn't turn around. Smirking, I watched until she was out of sight. Was I just talking to the white ninja? No way, right?

There's *no way*, right?

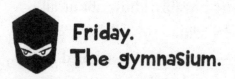 **Friday.**
The gymnasium.

The rest of the morning breezed by, mostly because I knew my friends were *still* my friends. Things might be awkward between Brayden and me, but hopefully that'd pass too.

I had eaten lunch by myself in the lobby since I didn't feel like getting food thrown at my face again.

As I stepped into the gymnasium, I realised that I hadn't seen Melvin all day. I was so distracted by my friends' forgiveness that I totally forgot he had an article to publish with my ugly mug at the top of it. There was no doubt he had pics of me getting unmasked by Jake.

It was the story he'd been hunting for all week. If I didn't at least try to explain myself to him, I'd regret it. Hopefully he'd be cool and not publish the article. If my life was bad *before* my secret was revealed, just imagine what it was going to be like afterwards.

Seriously, my parents would probably huddle together in the corner crying about where they went wrong, and where they could've tried harder. Or whether it was too late to put me up for adoption.

Chairs were set up at the front of the gym just like Monday's assembly, except there was one extra chair on the end with my name on it. I think they forgot Brayden had dropped out, which meant an empty seat between Zoe and me.

In front of the chairs, Principal Davis and some kids from the tech club were setting up a podium.

To the right of the podium was a huge red

machine that looked like something from a '70s
science-fiction movie. There was a slot in the
top and one on the side. Under the side slot
was a set of buttons that looked like they were
taken from an old arcade machine.

'Coopster for president!' shouted one of the
students as he took a seat on the bleachers. The
boys around him cheered my name too. I guess
not *everyone* in school hated me.

Some of the kids behind them were holding
signs with my name painted on them.

'Aren't you guys mad that I gave away
everyone's secrets?' I asked.

One of the blond boys stood and put his

hand on my shoulder. 'The school would be a better place if kids didn't keep secrets! Especially because I learned that the girl I had a crush on felt the same way.'

The girl next to him smiled at me.

'Oh, that's why you guys are cool with all that,' I said. 'You're all the kids who benefited from that gossip paper.'

Everyone in the section cheered together, but I couldn't bring myself to be happy with them. It still felt wrong. I waved, though. C'mon, when was the next time I was going to have any fans?

At the front of the gym, the other candidates were taking their seats. As I sped to join them, I spotted Naomi at the other end of the room, sitting in the first spot on the bleachers. She had been watching me the entire time, waiting for me to see her.

She raised her eyebrows at me. It was her way of giving me one final warning before assembly started.

All I had to do was take my place up the

213

front and keep my mouth shut. Daisy would win the election, the Scavengers would have their president, and I could just blend in until I graduate.

If you'd asked me at the beginning of the year if that sounded nice, I would've said yes. But things have been different for me in the past few months. Things have got better, and I've changed.

I didn't want to get lost in the crowd anymore.

I sat in my seat up the front, watching all the kids in the gym. Nearly every spot on the bleachers was taken.

Zoe leaned over the empty chair between us. 'This is exciting, isn't it? Soon we'll find out who the new president is!' She crossed her fingers, giggling. 'Listen, if *you* win, we're still cool, okay? I'd rather you win than Wyatt.'

Wyatt slouched forward to see past Daisy. 'Don't count on it, losers. Get used to hearing "President Wyatt" because that's all you're going to hear after today.'

'That doesn't make sense,' Zoe said, rolling her eyes.

'Yes it does!' Wyatt said.

Daisy said nothing, sitting perfectly still with her hands folded on her lap. She was staring into space. If it wasn't for her shoulders rising with each breath, I could've mistaken her for a porcelain doll.

I studied her, anxious for the assembly to start. She knew she was going to win this thing. It was promised to her by the Scavengers. It probably felt pretty good to be certain of victory.

'But if *I* win,' Zoe said, snapping me out of it, 'then I'd love it if you'd help me with my role. You fumbled this week when you couldn't be my campaign manager, but that's behind us.'

Zoe was so good at making me feel guilty without knowing it. She was being so cool by forgiving me and asking me to help after she won.

Too bad she wasn't going to win. Maybe that's why I felt terrible.

Oh well. For the sake of my ninja secret, it was time to push those emotions down to the deepest part of my stomach.

I looked around for Melvin. There were a lot of kids in the gym so I wasn't sure I'd even see him at all. It was like trying to find that guy in the red and white striped sweatshirt and hat – *frustrating and impossible*! What's he doing in overcrowded places to begin with?

Principal Davis strolled to the podium. He tapped the microphone twice and said, 'What's up, Buchanan Meese?'

Everyone cheered.

Tapping on the red machine next to the podium, the principal continued. 'In just a few

moments we're going
to use this vote counter
to print out the
results of the
election! This is the
BOJO 2015, a state-
of-the-art vote counter.'

I leaned towards my
cousin. 'Don't we need to vote first?'

Zoe looked at me like I was an idiot.
'Everyone voted during lunch. Didn't you?'

'Ugghhhh,' I groaned, sinking down like my
body was turning to mush.

'*You didn't vote?*' Zoe whispered harshly.

I smiled, but it was forced. 'Whoops.'

'Man, if I lose by *one* vote, I'm going to be
so upset with you!'

Leaning back in my chair, I stared at the red
machine that Principal Davis was resting his
arm on. How was Naomi going to rig the
election? They were using a machine to count
the votes, but was it possible that she found a
way to hack into it?

Daisy moved to the empty seat next to me.
'Hello, Chase.'

I glanced at Zoe, who was distracted
watching the crowd.

'Daisy,' I said, looking away.

'This will all be over shortly,' she said, bravely
speaking aloud while sitting between my cousin
and me. 'All you have to do is absolutely
nothing. That's easy for you, right?'

Her words cut into my heart.

'How's it feel to finally fail?' Daisy asked.

Now she was just twisting the knife.

'Leave me alone,' I said.

'Maybe after this I will. Or maybe I won't. Maybe this has been the most excitement I've had my entire life, and maybe I won't let up on you,' Daisy sneered. 'Maybe I've enjoyed watching you squirm as Naomi held you over the fire. And maybe this is just the beginning of a beautiful war between you and the Scavengers.'

'Maybe you say "maybe" too much,' I said.

'Maybe,' Daisy said.

Principal Davis slapped the top of the vote counting machine. It wasn't working properly – probably because it was such an ancient gadget.

I wanted to tell Daisy that she wasn't going to get away with this – that *none* of the Scavengers would – but what good was it? They were going to pull it off without anyone knowing any better. Anyone except me.

Even if I did say something, it's not like I had any proof. It's not like I could stand up in front of everyone and start telling them about the Scavengers and their plan to rig the election. The principal would look at me and be like, 'How do you know?'

And what would my answer be? 'I just know!' wasn't good enough. I would look like a crazy person, not to mention a sore loser since I was *in* the election!

The Scavengers seemed to have every corner covered, and it was sickening to me. No wonder why Naomi was such a good ninja – because she was an even better Scavenger.

Finally, the red machine spat out a long sheet of paper. Principal Davis caught it in the air. He squinted so he could read the fine print. A smile appeared on the principal's face as he tapped the microphone again.

Daisy had returned to her seat next to Wyatt. She was sitting straight up with her eyes half closed.

Wyatt was scanning his victory speech, moving his lips as he recited it to himself.

Zoe had her eyes squeezed shut. Her fingers were crossed as she held them next to her face, and her legs were bouncing up and down.

She wanted to win so badly. I had to look away from her because I knew what was about to happen. I didn't want to see the moment her heart broke.

Principal Davis let out a puff of air through his nose. 'Buchanan Meese, I'm pleased to present to you the winner of the election by a *landslide*...'

The crowd fell silent, eagerly awaiting the results.

Something had to happen, right? The bad guys don't win in situations like this, do they? My heart was pounding in my chest. Come on! Please say that someone else had won! I'd even accept *Wyatt* as president if it meant the Scavengers didn't win!

Principal Davis shouted loudly into the mic, 'Give a big round of applause for *President Daisy*!'

Zoe tried keeping her composure, but I saw her body sink ever so slightly. A smile appeared on her face, but I knew there was a world of sadness behind it.

I bit my lip as Daisy stood. She clapped both hands in front of her chest like a cheerleader.

Then she mouthed the words 'Thank you' as she started waving to the cheering crowd.

Balloons and confetti drifted down from the ceiling and music started playing over the sound system. The Scavengers had won and the presidency would remain in their clutches.

How? How could this have happened?

From the bleachers, I saw Naomi staring at me. Not angry – just staring. I'm not sure why, but the story of Gwen, the queen of Scrag Seven, started replaying in my mind.

The prisoner I had rescued on Scrag turned out to be not just the villain, but the ultimate villain – the *queen*. Someone I had trusted, someone who was helping me, someone who was fighting by my side and then *betrayed* me.

All of humanity was going to be enslaved if the queen wasn't stopped. And now Buchanan School was going to be led by another Scavenger.

I saved the Earth in the story by sacrificing myself, tackling the queen. Obviously tackling Naomi wasn't going to save the day, but...

My brain lit up as blood surged through my veins.

I could fix this.

I could change the election. I didn't have solid evidence, but if I told the school a secret so huge their minds exploded, then maybe, just *maybe* I could bring enough attention to the Scavengers that Principal Davis would *have* to investigate!

But it meant that I had to sacrifice myself.

The only power the Scavengers had over me was the fact that the school didn't know I was a ninja.

Well, that was about to change.

Daisy was at the centre of the gym, shaking hands and getting her picture taken when I walked up to the podium.

'Hello?' I said into the mic, checking to see if it was still on. My voice came through loud and clear over the speakers.

Principal Davis stood behind me. 'Chase, what're you doing?'

'I'd like to address the students,' I said. 'I'd

like to apologise for all the mess that's happened this week.'

The principal thought for a moment. 'I think that's appropriate, but keep it short.'

'Roger, roger,' I said, tapping the microphone with my finger. 'Um, hello?'

Everyone in the gym slowly fell silent. All eyes were on me. Even Naomi's. It was right at that moment I saw Melvin step through the doors.

Good. At least when he prints his story, everyone will be ready to believe it.

I cleared my throat, aware of the many eyes on me. Most of those kids hated me, but in just a few seconds they were going to hate me even more.

Was I about to do the dumbest thing I've ever done? This was a life changing decision that would follow me through to graduation. I'll be forever remembered as 'that weirdo ninja kid'.

Glancing to the side, I saw Zoe. And in that instant, I knew I was about to do the right thing.

Admitting to the school that I was a ninja was just the beginning. The domino effect would continue until the Scavengers were revealed, and then further until Daisy's victory was exposed as a lie. It was the right thing to do. There wasn't even an inch of me that thought otherwise.

'First of all,' I said, 'I'd like to apologise to everyone for any stress or heartache the *Chase Cooper Newsletter of Secrets* might've put you through. If I could go back in time and burn all those papers, I would.'

Naomi slowly lifted her head, listening

carefully. 'I know I'm normally the shy quiet guy who sits in the back of class. A few of you might recognise me from some bizarre antics I've been a part of since I started school here,' I said. 'I'll tell you exactly why I was involved in those antics. It's because I've been living two lives...'

I heard Wyatt squirm in his seat behind me.

Zoe gasped, and whispered, '*What are you doing?*'

But I ignored her and continued speaking. 'One life that everyone knows about is as a sixth grader at Buchanan, but the other life is a secret, filled with darkness and shadows...'

The gym was so silent that if I shut my eyes, I would swear it was empty. To make it easier, I actually *did* shut my eyes.

'You see,' I said, before pausing. My hands were trembling like leaves, and my knees felt like they had teleported away from my body.

I was about to do it. About to let the school know I was a ninja that had a secret ninja clan. About to take away all the power the Scavengers had over me. About to ruin my own life.

'You see,' I repeated, my voice shaking.
I took a deep breath. 'I'm a nin—'

'*Waaaait!*' screeched a voice in the gymnasium.

My heart was still in my belly when I squinted
to see who was running towards the podium.

It was Melvin. His brown loafers squeaked
on the floor as he stomped towards the front of
the gym, waving sheets of paper above his head.
'Stop! I have something to say!'

'I'm kind of in the middle of something,' I
said into the mic.

Melvin ignored me, pushing me away from the podium. Holding the papers over his head, he said, 'I have *proof* that Daisy rigged the election! She should not be president!'

'Those are pretty strong words,' Principal Davis said as he covered the mic with his hand.

Melvin held out the sheets of paper. They were photographs that he had taken when we were in the voting room. Daisy was in the background of the first picture, but the rest of the pictures were zoomed closer to see what she was actually doing.

Under his stack of photos were the pink slips that Melvin had taken from the voting room. They were the slips of paper that fell out of the box Daisy was holding over the red machine. The same red machine that was sitting next to the podium. The vote-counting machine.

'Tell me,' Melvin said, pointing to the results sheet that the red machine had printed. 'Does it say Daisy won because she got the vote of *every* homeschooled kid in the district?'

Principal Davis furrowed his brow, but checked the results like Melvin had asked. Then his expression softened. 'Yes. It does.'

'Those homeschooled kids don't exist!' Melvin said loud enough that his voice was carried through the speakers. 'Daisy rigged the election by winning a ton of votes from fake people! These pink slips are votes from homeschoolers, but when I looked them up, I found out they weren't even real! The machine makes sure that there aren't any duplicate names from any of the voters, but it doesn't count *similar* names as the same. Look!' Melvin pointed at the names on a couple of the pink slips. '*John* Doe. *Jon* Doe! I mean, come on, really? Daisy was dumping these votes into the voting machine *before* anyone even voted!'

Principal Davis was stone-faced as he studied the pink slips in Melvin's hand. Then he stepped up to the mic. With a calm voice, he said, 'Daisy, please go to the front office. I'll be there in a few minutes to have some words with you.'

I could hear gasps in the crowd. Whispers of how dead meat she was drifted through too.

Principal Davis stood in a huddle with several other teachers. They were whispering to each other and pointing at the photos and pink slips that Melvin had brought in.

I looked at the reporter who was leaning against the podium.

'Don't worry about it,' Melvin said, answering my 'thank you' before I even said it. He leaned away from the mic. 'You saved me yesterday. This was the least I could do for you.'

I nodded.

'Besides,' Melvin added, 'a rigged election is way more exciting than ninjas.'

Finally, Principal Davis took the podium again. 'I'm sorry to say that the results for the presidency were skewed, but after much discussion with the rest of the staff, we believe that the student who came in *second* place should be the winner. That and I think we're all so exhausted from this week that we just want to get a new president and move on.'

I stepped back and glanced at Zoe. In a fair election, she was definitely going to be the winner.

'Chase Cooper,' Principal Davis said, 'you received the second most votes, which makes you the president!'

My jaw dropped, and I think most of the kids felt the same. There were mixed reactions in the crowd. The section of students who were happy about the newsletter jumped to their feet, roaring with applause.

Principal Davis turned to me. 'But wait, what were you saying earlier? You're a nin-what?'

I paused, my jaw still hanging on its hinges. 'Nincompoop,' I said. 'I was *going* to say that I'm a nincompoop, and that I was going to respectfully bow out of the race.'

'I see,' the principal said. 'Well, since you're the winner, I'm sure you've changed your mind?'

I looked at Zoe. Now that Daisy was out of the way, I was going to be the president, but if *I* were out of the way, I knew the position would land on Zoe because I was sure Wyatt probably only got one vote, and that would've been from Olivia.

I'm sure you'd love to hear me say I made the 'right' choice, but to me, it was never a choice. Zoe *deserved* the presidency more than anyone in the entire school.

And she was the student who genuinely won. Daisy cheated. I was only elected because the Scavengers tossed my name into the hat. I shouldn't even have been in the race to begin with.

'No, sir,' I said to the principal, without taking my eyes off my cousin. 'I haven't changed my mind at all. I respectfully withdraw my name from the ballot.'

The principal rubbed the bridge of his nose, annoyed. 'Seriously, what's wrong with the kids at this school?' he mumbled. Then he scanned the voting results. He was too wiped to sound excited anymore. Leaning into the mic for a final time, he quickly said, 'Zoe is the new president of the school, and *that's* that.'

'I demand a recount!' Wyatt shouted as he stood.

The principal tossed the results to Wyatt. 'Count 'em yourself. You got zero votes.'

Wyatt studied the sheet of paper. '*Olivia* didn't even vote for me?'

Zoe threw her arms around me, almost knocking me to the floor. She was so happy that she couldn't say a word.

'You're welcome,' I said. 'I couldn't be there for you as a campaign manager, but I hope this makes up for that.'

She nodded. 'It does, but don't forget that I'm still going to need your help while I'm president so don't think you dodged a bullet with this.'

'I don't expect anything less from you,' I smirked.

Zoe took the podium and waved to the

crowd. They cheered loudly for her as she started giving her acceptance speech.

I looked over at Naomi, but she wasn't on the bench anymore.

Deep down, I knew that I had just declared war with the Scavengers, but I couldn't let myself think about it. There was too much to celebrate.

Melvin had a better story to print, and he wasn't going to reveal my secret. My friends were still my friends even after I was a butthead to them. And my cousin was the new president.

For such a disastrous week, it turned out better than I expected.

Without the presidency, the Scavengers were beginning to lose their grip on the school, and that felt awesome.

Even though my week was a double-decker bus of catastrophe, taking the Scavengers down a notch was worth it.

But I also knew that it wasn't the last time I'd run into them. They were able to wreck my life in less than a week, and I wasn't looking forward to seeing what they were capable of with more time.

As Zoe spoke about the future of Buchanan, I took my seat behind her, listening as she transformed into the leader she was born to be.

Daisy was somewhere in the principal's office by now.

Wyatt was off to the side of the gym, sitting next to Olivia, but they were facing away from each other. Wyatt was pouting with his arms folded as Olivia rolled her eyes.

Brayden was sitting with Gavin and Faith, clapping at Zoe's every other sentence.

Melvin was about a metre in front of the podium, taking photos of Zoe for the school paper.

Who knows where Naomi ran off to.

And me? I was perfectly happy being in the background as my cousin took the spotlight. Ninjas are at their best when they're neither seen nor heard. And at least for a little longer, my secret was safe.

My eyes caught Melvin's one last time. He nodded, and I returned the gesture.

The Scavengers *would* be back, I just didn't know when. It could be Monday, a week from now, a month from now. There was no sense in wasting time. If I wanted to be ready for them,

I'd have to start building a ninja clan, and soon. But this time I'd be more careful about who I picked. Melvin would be a good addition – reporters have the best connections.

I took a deep breath – deeper than normal. Then I held it for a second. Zoe had just said something that excited the school, and the gymnasium erupted with applause. The sound of cheering students flooded my ears, making it easier to clear my head. At last, I exhaled slowly, feeling all the weight from the week leave me.

Good thing it was Friday because my brain had just checked out for the weekend. All I wanted was to plop down in front of my video games with a stack of comic books by my side, drinking a frosty mug of orange soft drink with two scoops of vanilla ice cream in it. It might sound lame to you, but to me it sounded like the perfect weekend.

Zoe's speech was coming to an end. She said, 'I'm going to put in the hours and work weekends to be the best president I can be. I'm not even going to waste time telling all of you how I'll be different from Sebastian because I believe true leadership isn't about being better than the other guy…'

Um… was my own cousin about to steal my line?

Zoe winked at me, and continued. 'It's about always trying to be better than *yourself*.'

I laughed. Yup. She totally took that from me.

Diary of a 6th Grade Ninja series

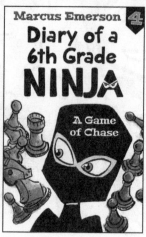

Collect
the
SET!

Marcus Emerson 5

Diary of a 6th Grade NINJA

Terror at the Talent Show

Marcus Emerson 6

Diary of a 6th Grade NINJA

Buchanan Bandits

Marcus Emerson 7

Diary of a 6th Grade NINJA

Scavengers

Marcus Emerson 8

Diary of a 6th Grade NINJA

Spirit Week Shenanigans

Marcus Emerson 9

Diary of a 6th Grade NINJA

Scavengers Strike Back

Marcus Emerson 10

Diary of a 6th Grade NINJA

My Worst Frenemy

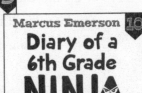

www.southdublinlibraries.ie
South Dublin Libraries

Marcus Emerson is the author of several highly imaginative children's books, including the 6th Grade Ninja series, the Secret Agent 6th Grader series, *Lunchroom Wars* and the Adventure Club series. His goal is to create children's books that are engaging, funny, and inspirational for kids of all ages – even the adults who secretly never grew up.

Marcus Emerson is currently having the time of his life with his beautiful wife and their amazing children. He still dreams of becoming an astronaut someday and walking on Mars.